"Sorry I'm late."
Verity opened the car door

"You don't look as though you're sorry," he grumbled, obviously set on a course of masochism.

"I don't look as though I'm a lot of things," she murmured, sounding unconsciously provocative.

"No. You don't. Why did you agree to work for me?"

"Because I need a job over the winter months, because I like France, because David asked."

"Do you always do what David asks?"

"No. Like you, Mr. McCaid, I don't do anything I don't choose to." Giving him a sweet smile that owed nothing to friendliness, she closed the door. "Shall we go?"

His answer was the overrevving of the engine before he catapulted the vehicle into the stream of traffic.

EMMA RICHMOND says she's amiable, undomesticated and an incurable romantic. And, she adds, she has a very forbearing husband, three daughters and a dog of uncertain breed. They live in Kent. A great variety of jobs filled her earlier working years, and more recently she's been secretary to the chairman of a group of companies. Now she devotes her entire day to writing, although she hasn't yet dispelled her family's illusions that she's reverting to the role of housekeeper and cook! Emma finds writing obsessive, time-consuming—and totally necessary to her well-being.

Books by Emma Richmond

Don't miss any of our special offers. Write to us at the following address for information on our newest releases.

Harlequin Reader Service
901 Fuhrmann Blvd., P.O. Box 1397, Buffalo, NY 14240
Canadian address: P.O. Box 603,
Fort Erie, Ont. L2A 5X3

EMMA RICHMOND

heart in hiding

Harlequin Books

TORONTO • NEW YORK • LONDON
AMSTERDAM • PARIS • SYDNEY • HAMBURG
STOCKHOLM • ATHENS • TOKYO • MILAN

Harlequin Presents first edition November 1990
ISBN 0-373-11317-X

Original hardcover edition published in 1989
by Mills & Boon Limited

CHAPTER ONE

WITH a warm smile at the hovering waiter, Verity took a chair at a vacant table and ordered milky coffee. There was only one other occupant of the pavement café, which wasn't exactly surprising in the first week of January, yet the air seemed to hold a soft reminder of summer, a fading memory of long, warm days. But then, that was partly why she liked France, the mildness of the winters. The other customer neither looked up from the newspaper he was reading, nor gave any indication at all that he was no longer alone, and Verity allowed her eyes to drift over him curiously. Most people glanced up or twitched at a noise, at the arrival of another. Not this man. This man seemed encased in his own private world. Overlong dark brown hair that looked as though it might not have seen a comb that morning, dark lashes that hid his eyes, a square, determined chin that showed a trace of stubble. Designer, or merely unshaven? Turning her head as the waiter brought her coffee, she gave another faint smile. Unwrapping the sugar, her eyes on her task, she suddenly became aware of being watched. Lifting her lashes, she stared into eyes as cold as an English winter sky. Neither blue nor grey, they were totally without expression. Then, apparently satisfied that he had her attention, he looked back down at his newspaper. And that told you, Verity Lang, she told herself humorously. Don't stare at strange men. With a quick glance at her watch, she drank her coffee; then, leaving a handful of *francs* in the little saucer with the bill, she hitched her bag back on her shoulder and got to her feet. With a last look at the man, a small, rueful smile tugging at her mouth, she went back to work.

Walking swiftly through the closed market, her dark brown hair bouncing healthily on her shoulders, she turned into the rue DeLong and pushed open the glass doors of the office building. With a smile at the *concierge*, she walked up the first flight of stairs and into her office. David, her boss, was lounging back in her chair, his feet on her desk. Looking pointedly at his feet, a glance he blithely ignored, she hitched her straight grey suit skirt up slightly and sat gracefully in the chair opposite.

'Have your coffee? he asked, his face full of amusement.

'I did,' she murmured. 'And very nice it was, too.'

'Bring me one back?'

'No—you go and get your own coffee. If you're too lazy to mend the percolator, you have to pay the price,' she said softly, her large brown eyes crinkling at the corners, her gaze, as always, disconcertingly direct.

'Hard, Verity. Very hard,' he murmured, which made them both laugh. If there was one thing Verity was not, it was hard.

'All your little lambs left?' she asked.

'Mm—all gone back to the hotel to pack,' he replied, then gave a wry grimace that made Verity laugh.

'Go on, you know you enjoy it, lording it over them all. Satisfied? I thought the course went very smoothly, and they all seemed quite confident they'd passed the exam, I thought it might present a problem, their having to come back after Christmas just to take it, but they seemed to cope.'

'Mm, I had a quick glance at the papers. I don't envisage too many problems, I have one or two reservations, but as usual I'll take your word for it that all will do well.'

'They will,' she stated positively, 'especially Montagne; he'll do very well,' mentioning the Spaniard who would go back to his own country to manage their branch of the American bank in Barcelona.

'Mm, Pity about Andro, though, dropping out at the last minute—how did you know he didn't want to finish the course? He never said, did he?'

'No.' She smiled.

'Then how?' he asked puzzled.

'I don't know. Truly.' She gave another of her slow smiles when he looked disgusted. 'It isn't so unusual, you know. Most women have intuition.'

'Not like yours, they don't. Aren't you ever wrong about people?'

'Of course. It isn't magical, or a trick, I don't look at their hands, eyes, ears, whatever and suddenly know. It's just intuition.' She shrugged, for she was unable to explain something that she didn't fully comprehend herself. 'I can't read thoughts or minds, it's just a feeling I get.' With a wide grin, she murmured, 'You should learn to trust your feelings, not your logic, my friend.'

'I've tried!' he said forcefully. 'It doesn't work.' Then, lifting his feet to the floor and sitting up straight, he smiled at her. 'I'll just have to keep using yours. Don't ever leave me, will you?'

'I wasn't thinking of it,' she said drily. 'I rather enjoy looking after your little lame ducks.' And she smiled when he snorted.

'Anything less like lame ducks I have yet to see. Most of them are arrogant, pompous little twits until you take them in hand. It never ceases to amaze me how a little slip of a thing like you, who looks so . . .'

'Ordinary?' she supplied.

'Well, yes—no, not ordinary, quiet, gentle-looking, a little Jenny Wren, and yet within a few hours of meeting them you have all the delegates eating out of your hand.'

'And it infuriates you and intrigues you and teases at your mind, wondering how on earth such a little brown mouse could wield such power,' she murmured softly. Tilting her head on one side so that she looked even more like the bird he had likened her to, she asked silkily, 'So what did you want to see me about? Not to discuss the finer points of my personality, I know.'

'How do you know I want to see you about anything?' he asked, amused.

'Because you wouldn't be sitting in my office, in my chair, if you didn't,' she pointed out. 'You're much too lazy to leave your own office unless there's a damned good reason.'

'Mm.' Putting his elbows on the desk and propping his chin in his hands, he stared at her, and when Verity raised her eyebrows in query he gave a lazy smile. 'Do you know what? I think you hypnotised me.' And when she gave a snort of laughter, he insisted, 'No, I'm sure you did. Why else would I have hired you? You had no banking qualifications, no experience of manager training, and I was going to turn you down flat at the interview, when you fixed me with those enormous eyes and I found myself giving you the job. Extraordinary. Must have been hypnotism, for how else would you persuade me utterly and convincingly that you could deal with twelve foreign delegates while I tried to instil information into their often unreceptive brains? Know that you could cope with their personal problems, wipe their noses, make sure they had the right notes . . .'

'Intuition?' she teased softly. Then, determined not to be sidetracked any more, she prompted softly, 'Which brings us to . . .?'

Laughing, he slumped back in the chair. 'Which brings us to the reason for my visit. You don't have anything lined up for the next couple of months, do you?'

'No,' she agreed, a fact he knew very well.

'No,' he echoed. 'I met an old friend last night . . .'

'Oh-ho,' she murmured, her face set in lines of resignation.

'And,' he went on determinedly, 'he's looking for someone to work for him for the next few weeks . . .'

'And one thing led to another,' she said drily.

'Well, you did say you didn't have anything planned . . .'

'And my services here will not be required until the beginning of April when the next new course starts. So, working on the principle that beggars can't be choosers, you offered my services.'

'Mm. So will you?' he asked, his grey eyes full of humorous entreaty.

'Doing what?'

'Oh, a bit of typing, answering the phone, getting rid of unwanted callers . . .'

'And?' she asked wryly, knowing from his

airy tone that there must be more. David at his most bland was David at his most outrageous.

'And nothing!' he exclaimed, which was a complete and utter lie. Verity could see from his face that he was being evasive. So, if it wasn't anything to do with his friend, he must have told him something about herself. 'So, what did you tell him about me?'

'Only that you don't get ruffled very easily, that you were good with people,' he said calmly.

'Why do I need to be good with people?' she asked softly. 'Difficult is he?'

'No! Well, not exactly,' he mumbled, 'only sometimes.' Then, spreading his hands in resignation, he added, 'You might find him a bit—er—cold. He doesn't say very much.'

'A bit like me?'

'No, not like you. His silences are more in the way of—er—bloody-mindedness, not because he's a quiet person. He doesn't suffer fools very gladly, either. In fact,' he added morosely, 'he doesn't suffer them at all. Especially at the moment; he's just getting over the flu.'

'He sounds wholly delightful,' murmured Verity. 'When do I get to meet this paragon?'

'I told him to come in about eleven-thirty—any time now, in fact,' he murmured, glancing at his watch. With a grimace, he let his breath out on a long sigh. 'To be honest, Verity, he can be an unmitigated bastard—perhaps it wasn't very wise to offer your services. Forget I asked,' he said, getting swiftly to his feet. 'It was a lousy idea. I'll tell him you're not free.'

'Very clever, David,' she applauded. 'Am I now supposed to be eaten up with curiosity? Beg to meet him?'

'No!' With a wide grin, David added, 'I suddenly decided it might be a bit like sending a lamb to the slaughter. Although he should consider himself damned lucky to get you!'

'But he won't,' she guessed.

'No. Although you would be truly excellent for him. You'd get rid of his unwanted callers with a charm that will make them think they've been flattered instead of rejected. You'll be able to sort out the genuine from the fake—he gets an awful lot of unsolicited calls, you know——' He broke off with such a look of horror that Verity stared at him in astonishment. Seeing her glance, he added hastily, 'Because he's—um— well-known and —er—wealthy. The wealthy always attract cranks . . .'

'Well-known?' she asked silkily. 'How well-known is well-known, David? An ageing rock star? Actor?'

'Corbin? Good lord, no!' he spluttered. Then, with a roar of laughter, he threw himself back into the chair, nearly tipping it over. 'Oh, heavens, Verity, wait till I tell him that!'

'David,' she said with barely suppressed exasperation, 'who is he?'

'Corbin McCaid.' And when she only looked at him in blank incomprehension he burst out, 'McCaid! The racing driver! Verity, you must have heard of him, He's the world champion! He . . . well, he's the world champion,' he muttered, and Verity narrowed her eyes at him. What on earth was going on? That was twice he'd broken off in the middle of what he was about to say, but before she could pursue it they both heard heavy footsteps sound along the corridor outside, and her attention was successfully diverted.

'By the pricking of my thumbs, something evil this way comes,' she said in a stage whisper, then gave a gurgle of laughter as David pulled a face. 'You know what will happen, don't you?' she asked with amusement. 'We'll walk into your office, he'll take one glance at me, look at you in disbelief and astonishment and shake his head slowly at the stupidity of his friend.'

'Well, he might at first,' he admitted cautiously, 'but not when he's seen you in action . . .' He broke off as Verity chuckled infectiously.

'Action man I am not, David, nor ever likely to be.' Getting to her feet, she tugged her suit jacket straight. 'Come along, then, let's get it over with.'

With a sigh, David got to his feet. Linking his hand in the crook of her elbow, he escorted her along to his office. With a humorous look at her he pushed his door wide—and there he was. The man from the café. Old sober-sides, except of course that he wasn't old. He looked no warmer, no more approachable than he had half an hour ago. With his back to the window his face looked darker, his eyes brighter, and as they travelled over her his mouth curved cynically.

'Ah,' he said cryptically—and she knew exactly what he was thinking: that she had known who he was and had sat in the café to give him the once over. Her eyes amused, she slowly shook her head.

'Wrong,' she said softly, not that he looked as though he believed her, but then he didn't look the sort of man who believed very much at all. Moving his eyes away from her, he gave David a brief nod of greeting. He was taller than David, she noted, as her boss went to stand beside him, and leaner. And where David's face was open and humorous, this man's was wary, distrustful—and sneering, she decided. This man had sneering down to a fine art.

'How are you feeling?' David asked.

'Fine,' he said abruptly, but he wasn't, Verity thought; he was feeling lousy, only nothing on earth would make him admit it, not in front of her anyway. Neither would he sit down, or relax against the wall. She knew that too. Why? she wondered. What made it imperative for him to appear hard, in control? As David turned and extended a hand towards her, she walked gracefully across to them.

'Verity, this is Corbin McCaid; Corbin, Verity Lang.' And she gave a small nod, almost an exact replica of the one he had given David. He wouldn't shake hands, she knew, so kept her own by her sides. She found she knew a lot about this man without knowing him at all. Not that it mattered what he was like, she could cope with him, whatever his moods. She always coped, and would be whatever he wanted her to be—that was her stock in trade. A chameleon, she often thought of herself, a succession of characters, all playing a part. And who was the real Verity? Somewhere buried inside was presumably the person she should have been, would have been, if fate, circumstance, destiny, whatever, had played a different tune.

Corbin had taken an instant aversion to her, his face showed that very clearly; or maybe it wasn't her, exactly, but anyone he was forced to ask a favour of. But then, she didn't need him to like her, any more than she needed to like him. She needed a job for the next few months, and the prospect of working for him was as good, or bad, as any other. No, better, she mentally corrected, because then she could stay in France.

When it became obvious that no one else was going to say anything, she said the first thing that came into her head. 'David said you have flu, Mr McCaid.'

'Had,' he corrected harshly, and she gave a small smile. Yes, *had,* she silently agreed; even flu would not dare linger too long on that hard body.

'David also said,' she persevered, 'that you wanted someone to work for you for a few months.'

'Yes. Someone—not necessarily you, Miss Lang.'

'No,' she echoed softly, not one whit put out by his rudeness, 'not necessarily me.'

'You couldn't do better,' David said, treading clumsily in.

'Couldn't I?' he asked softly, clearly not believing it for a minute. 'And what makes you so special? Just who the hell are you, Verity Lang?'

'Whoever you want me to be,' she answered simply, her eyes full of laughter.

'Very clever. Perhaps you would now care to explain just exactly what that means?'

'It means, whatever you want me to be, I will be.' Then she had an absurd desire to burst into a soaring rendition of 'Che Sera Sera', and her generous mouth twitched slightly.

'Quiet is what I want you to be. Unobtrusive.'

'Then that's what I'll be,' she murmured, her eyes too wide and innocent to be true. Heaven knew, she'd had enough practice at being what people wanted. Her parents had died when she was eleven, and after that she had gone to live with the dreaded Aunt Lucy and her overpowering offspring, who had considered it their reluctant duty to instruct her in the ways of the world—and, if there was one word that Verity hated more than any other, it was duty. But she had learned to conform to whatever standards were required of her. It hadn't always been easy, but she had learned. If she was to be meek, then she was meek; if vivacious, then vivacious, not that her aunt had ever wanted that. But meek, unobtrusive—oh, yes, those she had learned very well.

'You can type?'

'Yes.'

'Presumably answer the phone, take messages . . .'

'Yes.'

'Be discreet?'

'Oh, yes—a veritable clam, truly,' she answered, amused, and he was hating it—oh, how he was hating it. Why?

Staring at her for long moments, his empty eyes searched hers. 'I live alone,' he said abruptly, and she gave a little nod.

'You need someone to cook and clean and sew?' she asked softly, and *he* gave a little nod, a brief flash of—was that amusement in his eyes? David, she saw, was looking totally bewildered, and she gave him a small smile. Leave it, she told him silently, this is way beyond your head. Corbin was warning her not to encroach on his preserves—and she was warning him that she wasn't as soft as she looked. The message was understood by both.

'I'll give you a week's trial. When can you start?'

'Saturday,' both she and David said together.

'Friday,' he corrected arrogantly. 'Noon. I'll wait for you outside—don't keep me waiting.' With an impartial nod at them both, he walked out. The door closed very softly behind him.

A rather pregnant silence reigned in the
office for a good few minutes after he'd left.
Then, turning to David, Verity fixed him with
an unwavering stare. 'And just what were you
both carefully not telling me? Well? And you
can take that look of spurious innocence off
your face, David Morse.'

'I don't know what you mean,' he blustered,
'and if anyone's not telling anyone anything,
it's you. What was all that moody exchange of
glances all about?'

'Lines of demarcation,' she said softly.
'Now your turn.'

Giving a humphing sigh, he muttered, 'Only
that—well, should his mother turn up, you
have to pretend to be in love with him.'

'I have to *what?* Oh, come on, David,' she
muttered in disgust. 'Pull the other one.'

'No, truly, he . . .'

'David, that man looks as though he'd sell
his grandmother's bath-chair if the price was
right, so don't tell me he can't deal with his
mother!'

'You haven't met her,' he said morosely. 'I
mean, she's the dearest soul, but . . .' Sighing
again, he stared at her helplessly. 'Oh, damn
Corbin. Why do I always get involved in his
crazy schemes?'

'Are you sure we're both talking about the
same man?' she asked wryly. 'Corbin McCaid
didn't look as though he'd know a crazy

scheme if he fell over one. So come on, why must I pretend to be in love with him?'

'Because his mother keeps trying to introduce him to what she considers desirable females, and it's driving him to distraction—and I said you were very good with mothers,' he muttered, almost inaudibly.

'David!'

'Well, you're good with my mother.'

'Which is hardly the same thing, I suspect. Well, why doesn't he just tell her to get lost? No, I know,' she tacked on impatiently when he opened his mouth, 'I haven't met his mother. All right, let's try another tack. Why does his mother think he needs help finding a female?'

'Well, I don't know, do I?' he demanded. Only he did, Verity saw that very clearly and, although David was usually the most amiable of souls, there were occasions when he dug in his heels and refused to budge. This was obviously one such occasion, she decided.

'All right, then, mothers and my ability to deal with difficult people apart, why specifically me?'

'Because you speak both English and fluent French . . .'

'So do a lot of other people . . .'

'Will you stop interrupting? I know a lot of other people do, but he doesn't know any and neither do I. Nor,' he added firmly when she tried to interrupt again, 'does he want to use an agency. He wants someone he can trust, someone who'll keep their mouth shut about what he's doing.'

'What is he doing?'

'Verity! He'll tell you that himself. And no, it isn't illegal, just something he doesn't want talked about. He also,' he continued with the air of a man sorely tried, 'doesn't want some daffy female who's likely to fall in love with him . . .'

'Hah!'

'Exactly,' he said triumphantly. 'If there is one person I know who has never to my knowledge drooled over a male, it's you.'

'I could always start,' she taunted softly, then grinned when he slapped her arm. 'But you never know, David,' she murmured, her serious tone belied by the twinkle in her eyes, 'he might be the very man to crack the ice.'

'I very much doubt it,' he said drily. 'And if he does, I'd be enormously grateful if you'd suppress it. I want you back in one piece in April.'

Shaking her head at him, she turned to go back to her own office. 'The whole thing seems utterly crazy to me—still, as you so rightly pointed out, I do need to work over the winter months . . .'

'It's also a challenge, eh, Verity? And you do so love a challenge . . .'

Laughing, she went back to her office to finish off typing the last report on the delegates. Her mouth still curved in a smile, she plumped down in her chair and swung it round to stare out of the window. 'Well, Mr Corbin McCaid, I hope you know what you've taken on.' Chuckling, she turned determinedly back to her desk.

Friday, midday, found her still frantically typing. David had mislaid some of his notes, and would she mind retyping them? She still had the files to pack away so that they could be taken back to the head office of the European branch of the bank in London, and she was very conscious of Corbin sitting outside the office in a dark blue Mercedes. She could almost feel the waves of temper wafting up to her third floor office. Ripping the last page out of her typewriter, she handed it to David.

'Right. Thanks, Verity.' Adding the page to the pile on the edge of the desk, he walked across to the window and peered out. 'Oh, hell, he's outside. Are you nearly ready?'

'I know he's outside,' she said shortly, 'and no, I'm not, I still have the files to pack up.'

'Well, don't let's panic . . .'

'I'm not. You are—anyone would think you were terrified of him.'

'Don't be ridiculous!' Then, giving her a shamefaced grin, he confessed, 'I am. Corbin in a temper is something to be avoided at all costs.'

'Oh, now he tells me!' she exclaimed wryly as she hastily removed the files from the cabinet and stacked them in the cardboard box on the floor.

'Are you packed?'

'Yes, David—and yes, I have checked out of the hotel—no, I do not need any money—yes, I have a clean hanky.'

With a snort of laughter he slapped her hands away from the files. 'I'll finish these, you get along.'

'Thanks,' she said gratefully. 'I'll just have a quick wash, then I'll be off.' Whipping along to the Ladies, she washed her hands and combed her unruly hair before walking swiftly back to the office, Automatically checking that nothing had been left, she took her sheepskin off the coat-stand. 'Right,' she declared. 'You'll let me know the venue for April?'

'Mm, almost certainly Rome, but I'll keep in touch.' Walking across to her, he smiled down into her face. 'Take care, hm? I'll see you as and when.'

'All right, and thank Mary again for having me at Christmas, won't you?' With a last look round, she picked up her suitcase and handbag and went down to the waiting car, and the no doubt bad-tempered Corbin McCaid.

'You're late,' he said crossly as she opened the passenger door.

'I know. I'm sorry,' she apologised quietly as she hoisted her case into the back seat.

'You don't look as though you are,' he grumbled, obviously set on a course of masochism.

'I don't look as though I'm a lot of things,' she murmured, sounding unconsciously provocative.

'No. You don't. Why did you agree to work for me?'

'Because I need a job over the winter months, because I like France, because David asked.'

'Do you always do what David asks?'

'No. Like you, Mr McCaid, I don't do anything I don't choose to.' Giving him a sweet smile that owed nothing to friendliness, she closed the door and slotted her seat-belt into place. 'Shall we go?'

Her answer was the over-revving of the engine before he catapulted them into the traffic with scant regard for anybody's safety.

CHAPTER TWO

'WHERE are we?'

'I haven't the faintest idea.'

'Well, you're the bloody navigator!' he exploded.

'Mr McCaid, I can't read road signs and the map at the same time; be reasonable. No, cancel that, being reasonable is obviously a physical impossibility.'

'Right, that's it!' he gritted, slamming the car to a halt. 'You drive, I'll navigate! You can drive, I take it?'

'Oh, yes, Mr McCaid, I can drive.' Giving him a look that might have stripped paint if he'd been looking at her, which he wasn't, she opened her door to climb out, and the interior light illuminated his face for a moment. He looked grey, and she belatedly remembered that he'd had flu. 'Had' being the operative word.

'Are you intending to stand there all night?' he asked rudely, and any sympathy she might have felt fled. Closing the door with a careful precision that was far more telling than a slam, she walked round to the driver's side as Corbin shuffled across the seat. Ah, but gallantry is not dead, she thought with a spurt of amusement. The lady climbs out in the rain, the man stays warm and dry. Climbing behind the wheel, she stared at the dashboard clock. Seven p.m. They should have been on the outskirts of Auray by now. Paris to Auray would take six hours, David had said. Hah! At the rate they were going, they'd be lucky to get there by tomorrow! Fitting the seat-belt firmly in the slot, she put the car in gear.

'Take the next road on the right,' he said authoritatively.

'Certainly,' she murmured. Driving slowly, she peered hopefully at wet hedgerows, then more wet hedgerows, a soggy field. There appeared to be no signposts, no cottages, villages, no nothing. Goodness only knew where they were. She didn't even remember seeing any of the little yellow route numbers that usually spattered the French roads—but she wouldn't say anything. Oh, no. He was the navigator. Turning the wipers to 'fast' to cope with the sudden deluge of rain, she concentrated on her driving.

Could silences be thunderous? she pondered some half-hour later. Certainly his seemed to be, and if he tapped his fingers just once more on the open mapbook she thought she would quite likely hurl it through the window. And wouldn't you just know it? The moment her concentration lapsed, a crossroads suddenly appeared out of nowhere and Verity had to brake to a frantic stop.

'Did you see what the sign said?'

'No. I'm not entirely capable of reading signs

that flash past at ninety miles an hour,' he muttered sarcastically.

'Don't exaggerate, Corbin,' she reproved gently. 'I was doing no more than thirty.'

'Really?' Slamming the book on the parcel shelf, he opened his door and climbed out, and she gave a little grin as he ostentatiously turned up the collar of his jacket and walked back to the signpost. They'd been doing so well too, until they'd got to Rennes, that was. That was where their present troubles had started, along with the rain. The signs for Vannes had mysteriously disappeared, and she hadn't been quick enough finding alternative towns on the map in the direction they wanted before Corbin had shot off down a road that he'd insisted was in the right direction, and unfortunately wasn't. The more she'd tried to tell him he was going the wrong way, the crosser he'd become. What they should have done was return to Rennes and start again. Only he wouldn't.

'You'll have to reverse,' he muttered, climbing back in. 'Then hang a right, that should take us to Gacilly. Then, according to the map,' he mumbled, peering at it, 'we should be able to get to Ploermel and back on the road to Vannes.'

' "Should" being the operative word,' she murmured softly. 'Want to lay bets?'

'No, I do not. Just drive, Miss Lang.'

Miss Lang drove.

They eventually arrived on the outskirts of Auray

at gone midnight. It had taken them ten hours—admittedly, they'd stopped in Vannes for something to eat, and then Corbin had again taken over the driving, but even so . . . He also drove very fast.

'Corbin! It's not the Grand Prix,' she'd felt forced to exclaim when the needle had actually gone off the speedometer.

'What's that supposed to mean?'

'It's not supposed to mean anything!' she'd said in exasperation. 'Don't be so damned touchy!'

'What did David tell you?' he demanded.

'About what?'

'About me, dammit!'

'Nothing,' she said shortly. 'Why should he? He merely told me you were a racing driver—no, I tell a lie,' she added sarcastically. 'He also said you were world champion! Is that what this is all about? I'm not giving you the deference you're used to, and so very obviously expect?'

'Don't be so stupid!' he muttered, and she looked at him in astonishment. He'd sounded almost embarrassed. Shrugging, she turned her attention to the scenery. Not that she could see much, only her reflection thrown back at her.

Naturally, Auray, when they reached it, was in darkness, all sensible people having gone to bed. The rain decided it had a lot more raining to do, and that it had better hurry up and get rid of its load before the windscreen wipers decided they could actually cope with the violent downpour of water. Peering intently through the windscreen, Verity watched out for the signs he said they must follow to get to the harbour. The streets were impossibly narrow, the cobbles slippery beneath the tyres, and with no streetlights to guide them the whole thing became a nightmare. Her head ached, her back ached and her left leg had gone to sleep. She'd been to Auray before, but that had been in the summer, in daylight. By night, and in the pouring rain, it looked different. Terrified of missing the turning and bringing more retribution down on her head, she finally directed him across the narrow bridge over the river. They crawled past the medieval houses, art galleries and cafés, which in the summer were full of tourists, and which now looked ghostlike, abandoned.

He parked beside the closed *crêperie,* muttering, 'I won't get the car up that narrow cobbled alley.'

'No,' she murmured tiredly. She'd already seen for herself that the car was too wide. Did he think she was blind? Probably.

'Do you have an umbrella?' he asked abruptly.

'Yes, I have an umbrella,' she confirmed, her voice as abrupt as his as she leaned over into the back seat to get it. 'David told me to pack for all eventualities.' Obviously he'd had some idea of what the journey was going to be like. It was a pity he hadn't shared his premonitions with her.

As he opened the car door to get out, Corbin gave a disagreeable sigh. 'Is it usually this damned wet here?'

'No, Britanny is usually very mild—and dry. I hope the gods aren't trying to tell us something,' she murmured forebodingly.

'Miss Lang,' he replied, not altogether humorously, 'if you turn out to be fey, on top of everything else, you can go back to Paris!' Turning his collar back up, he pushed the door wide and climbed out, and Verity hastily followed him, fighting to put the umbrella up in the lashing wind and rain. Not that he waited to make use of its protection; he just strode up the tiny cobbled alley.

'Well, don't wait, dear,' she grumbled, beginning to have serious doubts about the wisdom of even going to inspect the house. The way their luck was running, it would be inhabited by rats. He'd rented the house sight unseen in Paris, or so David had said; always a mistake she thought, to rent something on someone else's say so.

Hugging her sheepskin tightly around her, she set off after him, her boots slipping on the wet cobbles. There were no lights, no welcoming glow from behind rain-lashed windows, only dark, angry sky and the eerie moan of the wind between the crumbled ruins of houses waiting to be renovated. But then, January was hardly the best time to play tourist. The whole place looked like a film set for a horror movie, she decided, glancing warily round her as the alley narrowed yet further, or a Dickensian backdrop for Fagin's hideout. All it needed now was a visit from the undead. Twenty-five she might be, but that didn't make her immune from irrational fears of ghouls and ghosties. No matter what they said, they weren't the prerogative of children. She wasn't totally enamoured of the sound effects, either: thunder rumbling menacingly in the distance, water gurgling along the inadequate gutters, the echo of her own hurrying footsteps. No, she wasn't enamoured of it at all, although at least Corbin had had the presence of mind to bring a torch. Then she gave a screech of alarm as her foot went into a hole and she sprawled full-length on the wet cobbles.

'Damn!'

'What?' he shouted, turning hastily so that the torch beam wavered drunkenly. 'Oh, for pete's sake, Verity! Why the hell can't you look where you're going? Hasn't the day been bad enough, without you breaking your damned ankle?'

'No, I thought it had been so bloody boring, I'd liven it up somewhat!' she yelled furiously. 'Well, don't just stand there gawping! Give me a hand up!' Honestly, some people! she thought.

When he'd hauled her unceremoniously to her feet and given her a cursory glance to make sure she wasn't injured, he strode off again and she stuck her tongue out childishly at his back. Brushing the worst of the muck from her coat, she followed slowly after him. When he stopped to fit the key into a narrow doorway that didn't even seem to stand up straight, she huddled close behind him, her umbrella held to one side.

Heavens, what a day.

'Verity,' he muttered impatiently, 'how the hell am I supposed to get the key in the lock with you crowding me?'

'Sorry,' she mumbled. 'Here, give me the torch.' Taking the heavy-duty torch, she held its welcoming beam on the door as he fiddled with the old-fashioned lock. As he pushed the door wide with a protesting squeak of hinges, Verity finally and forever abandoned thoughts of comfort.

'Oh, hell,' she muttered as a cloying smell of damp wafted out to them.

Corbin's sentiments were a little more forceful as he depressed the light switch and one naked bulb vaguely illuminated the dreadful interior. A sewer would have had more homely qualities. She doubted whether any self-respecting rat would even give this place more than a fleeting glance. One twitch of his whiskers and he'd be off.

'Damn that agent!' Corbin exploded furiously. Wrenching the torch out of her hand, he pushed open the door on their left, then swore as he nearly fell over a pile of rubbish that had been left just inside, and Verity winced as he kicked furiously at it and sent it flying in all directions across the filthy floor. The light in this room didn't work at all, despite Corbin flicking the switch on and off in temper, which was maybe just as well; Verity had seen more than enough in the torch beam. There was no furniture, not even a stool, and naked floorboards were covered in newspaper and other rubbish that Verity had no wish to investigate.

'Well, that's it! We'll have to walk back into the town. There must be something we can rent for the night. We certainly can't stay here.'

'Are you sure we're in the right house?' she asked tentatively.

'No, I'm not bloody sure!' he growled. 'There are no damned numbers on the houses!'

'Well, what's the address? Maybe we're in the wrong road or something . . .'

'I don't have an address! He gave me explicit directions . . .' And he sounded so defensive that Verity guessed he'd had the address and lost it. 'Left-hand side,' he muttered, staring down at the soggy piece of paper attached to the key, 'house with brown front door.'

Without waiting for her to comment, he turned and stormed out, and with a sigh Verity followed him. Ho hum, she thought drearily. Well, she couldn't say she hadn't been told it might be a challenge.

Not bothering to put the umbrella back up, she hurried to catch up with Corbin's long strides as he walked further up the hill and stopped before another house. As he pushed open the door and snapped on the light, she peered over his shoulder.

'Well, thank heavens for that,' she muttered.

'Amen.'

The front door opened straight on to the living-room, a small precarious-looking staircase leading upwards, and, although it was apparent the house hadn't been actually cleaned ready for their arrival, it wasn't too bad, and she guessed it had been rented out the summer before to tourists. There was a pile of kindling beside the grate and a broom stood in the corner as though it were waiting, and Verity had a sudden vision of Mickey Mouse in *The Sorcerer's Apprentice,* commanding the broom to sweep. She hastily straightened her face as Corbin gave her an odd look.

'Well, at least we can sit down,' she remarked, indicating the sofa.

'And write?' he asked drily, walking across to the small table and two chairs.

'And be warm,' she murmured, moving to touch her boot lightly against the pile of firewood. Home sweet home it was not, but at least it was dry, and a hell of a lot better than tramping round Auray looking for alternative accommodation. 'Perhaps you can get the fire going while I investigate, see if anyone left provisions.'

As he muttered something she didn't quite catch, she pushed open the door set in the furthest wall. Kitchen, she discovered. Large, fairly well-equipped, with a door leading out to an open field. She could just make out the river glinting in the distance. Shivering, she hastily turned her attention to the cupboards. They were mostly full of cooking utensils, plates, cups—but no food. Walking back into the lounge, she watched Corbin for a moment. He'd removed his anorak and was bending before the fireplace, grumbling irritably to himself as he tried to persuade the wood to catch.

'Shall I go and get the suitcases?' she asked quietly.

Turning abruptly, as though she had startled him, he shook his head and got to his feet.

'I'll get the suitcases—perhaps you'll have more luck with the fire.' Shrugging back into his anorak, he went out, and the door was slammed very hard behind him.

'Oh, dear.' Surveying the miserable-looking fire, she had a sudden memory of her father crouching before an enormous fireplace, a mischievous grin on his face as he held a newspaper across the fire to draw it. Could almost hear the faint, humorous voice of her mother as she remonstrated with him, told him not to be stupid. With a little smile, she quickly went into the kitchen and picked up the folded newspaper she had found earlier in one of the cupboards. Walking back to the lounge, and foolishly looking round her as though someone might be watching, she knelt and held the paper up, then grinned as she heard the satisfying whoosh of the wood catching. When the paper got too hot to hold, she cautiously lowered it, then smiled rather smugly. 'Thanks, Dad.' Hearing the front door slam, she started and turned.

'Very clever, Verity,' he said shortly.

'Although it was no more than I should have expected.'

'What?' she asked puzzled.

'The fire, Verity. The fire.'

'You're angry because I managed to get it going and you couldn't?' she exclaimed in astonishment. 'Oh, come on, Corbin. I've come to accept the bad temper, don't be childish as well!'

'I'm not being childish,' he gritted, dumping both cases and a bag of golf clubs on the floor. Dragging off his soaking anorak, he tossed it on top of his case.

'Yes, you are—sulky and objectionable,' she said reasonably. 'It's not my fault we got lost. Things could have been a hell of a lot worse, you know. We'll just have to make the best of it.'

'I am not sulking!' he grated. 'I'm . . .'

'Yes, you are,' she continued in the same patient tone. 'You're behaving like a small boy deprived of his favourite toy.'

'Oh, am I!'

'Yes. Why on earth do men always get in a temper when things go wrong?'

'Men?' he exclaimed almost violently. 'Men get in a temper?'

'Yes,' she insisted.

'And I suppose you're not!'

'Of course I'm not. Do I sound as though I am? Although it wouldn't be any wonder if I was, would it? Not many people would put up with the kind of behaviour I've been putting up with all afternoon.'

'No, they wouldn't! They'd have said something earlier, instead of suffering in pained silence! Do you know how damned infuriating that is? Silent martyrdom?'

'Martyred? Well, I like that! Admittedly I was a little peeved . . .'

'Peeved?' he exclaimed. 'You were martyred!'

Getting slowly to her feet, she stood in front of him, her face reflecting her complete astonishment. 'I was not being martyred, Corbin—I was trying to be tolerant!'

'Tolerant? *Tolerant*?' he exploded. 'Waves of disapproval were coming off you like Niagara Falls!'

'They were not!'

'Yes, they were! Why the hell can't you just admit to getting in a temper like everybody else, instead of wrapping it up in fancy names? *Tolerant*,' he bit out in disgust. 'You were in a temper then—and you're in a temper now!'

'I am not!' she denied, feeling a strong desire to kick his shins, 'I do not have a temper, remember?' she grated, her jaw aching with the effort to remain controlled. 'Calm, competent, able to cope with all situations—David said so.'

'Then you're either a very good actress—or David was suffering from delusions!'

'Probably delusions,' she bit out, her own temper simmering nicely. 'And you the fool for believing him!'

'Hah! Trust a woman to turn it all round so

that it ends up my fault.'

'I didn't say it was anybody's fault,' she said through her teeth, 'I said I wasn't in a temper!'

'You are now,' he said, sounding almost triumphant.

'I am not!' she yelled.

'Aren't you?' he queried silkily. 'Then perhaps you'd be kind enough to explain just what happened to the oh, so calm, competent Miss Lang? Because she sure as hell isn't standing in front of me right now!'

Staring at him, her eyes narrowed to slits, her hands clenched by her sides, she gritted, 'She went out!' Swivelling on her heel, she stormed out to the kitchen and slammed the door. Grinding her teeth together in fury, she banged her hands down flat on the work surface. 'Ouch, that hurt,' she muttered, then gave a snort of laughter. Oh, boy, the pair of them had been behaving like children. Shaking her head in wry self-mockery, she walked quietly back to the lounge. Corbin was standing where she had left him, staring moodily down into the fire. His dark hair was still plastered wetly to his head, rivulets of water dripping to darken his sweater.

'I'm sorry, Corbin,' she murmured softly. 'I don't normally behave like this.' Then, with a little laugh, she added, 'It must be you . . .'

'Oh, I might have known it would be my doing!'

Laughing more naturally, she went to her case to get a towel. Rubbing her hair as dry as she could, she handed it to him with a little bow. 'Miss Lang will be back tomorrow,' she promised. 'Come on, dry yourself off before the flu you haven't got turns to pneumonia. I'll make us some coffee, if I can get the stove to work, that is.'

'We don't have any coffee, do we?'

'Oh, yes, we do. The competent Miss Lang brought some with her.' Going back to her case, she took out the polythene bag containing coffee, packets of sugar and powdered milk. 'I always keep some in hotel rooms because they never leave enough.'

Walking back to the kitchen, she put some water on to heat. Taking two mugs out of the cupboard, she made the coffee and carried it into the lounge. Corbin was now slumped on the sofa, and she gave a small smile. Poor Corbin! Instead of his problems lessening, they seemed to have trebled.

'A good night's sleep will work wonders,' she murmured bracingly as she handed him his coffee. 'Everything will look much better in the morning, you'll see.'

'Want to bet?' he asked softly.

Pulling a face at him, she yawned widely. 'I'm going to investigate the sleeping arrangements. I intend to get the best bed!'

Putting her coffee on the little table, she walked across to the rickety-looking staircase, and with a grimace cautiously put her foot on the first step. It creaked alarmingly. Giving Corbin a wry look as he got to his feet, she advanced carefully, hoping he'd have the good sense to wait until she got to the top before following her.

Opening the first door she came to, her heart sank as the distinct smell of damp came to her. Walking across to the unmade bed, she put her hand on the mattress. Damp, 'Oh, hell. It looks like one of us will have to use the sofa. No problem.'

'Not for you, no,' he said drily, 'because I know exactly who'll be using it.'

Turning to give him a wide grin of agreement, she walked along the landing to the next bedroom. Surely both beds wouldn't be damp? Opening the door, she stared into a small storage cupboard. 'Oh, how stupid!' she muttered, then actually walked inside to be absolutely certain her eyes weren't playing her tricks.

'No, I am not sleeping in the cupboard,' Corbin said softly from behind her.

'Did I ask you to?' she asked waspishly. The whole thing was getting beyond a joke.

'Not yet, but I have a feeling it's next on the agenda.'

'Don't be ridiculous,' she muttered. 'You said there were two bedrooms . . .'

'No, I didn't. I said I *thought* there were two bedrooms, a subtle difference.'

Pushing him impatiently out of the way, she brushed past him and walked further along the landing. Shoving open the end door, she stared in horrified fascination. It looked like the municipal dump. A twisted old bedstead on its side, a box of overflowing rubbish, a mouldy mattress—and a bicycle frame.

'Oh, well, that'll be useful,' she commented disgustedly. 'What the hell is a bicycle frame doing here?'

'How should I know?' he asked drearily.

'Well, we'll both have to use the sofa,' she said flatly. 'And no smart remarks, thank you, Corbin.'

'Oh, I wouldn't dream of it, not to the calmly competent Miss Lang, she'd probably brain me. How David thought you gentle and mild beats me. Personally, I think the whole thing is a ghastly mistake, and you'd do better to find another job for the remainder of the winter.'

She was begining to think that herself.

'Did you see any blankets on your tour of inspection?' he asked over his shoulder as he led the way down.

'No.'

'There's a rug in the car,' he said fatalistically. 'I'll go and get it.'

Reaching the bottom of the staircase, he suddenly stopped so that Verity barged into his back. 'Did you see a bathroom?' he demanded.

'What? Oh, hell, Corbin, don't even think it. There must be one; if it's rented out to tourists, then it has to have all the facilities.'

'Well, please don't tell me it's at the bottom of the garden. I couldn't bear it, not in this rain.'

'There isn't a garden, only a damned great

field,' she muttered absently. Staring round her, she suddenly stepped past him and walked to the door beside the front door which she had assumed was a cupboard. Pulling open the door, she gave a sigh of relief. 'Bathroom.'

When he'd gone, she took toothbrush, tooth-paste and a dry towel out of her case and went to wash. The water was freezing, as she might have expected; there was probably an immersion heater somewhere, if one only knew where the switch was.

Going back to the lounge, she hastily went to the fire to warm herself. Dragging off her boots, she put them tidily side by side, then perched on the edge of the sofa.

'You were a long time,' she murmured as Corbin came in. 'I was beginning to wonder if I ought to come and look for you. There is water, but it's cold and I couldn't be bothered to warm any up,' she added apologetically.

'Thanks,' he said drily. 'I'll go and make use of it. I'd hate you to think I hadn't been brought up properly.' And she gave him a look of irritation. She knew he was tired and probably feeling grotty, but really it would be better if he would just shut up. She thought she preferred the cold, distant man she had met in David's office.

'When did you say Miss Lang would be back?' he asked with soft sarcasm, and she wondered whether he'd picked up her thoughts, or his were just running on similar lines. Whatever, she was too tired for smart answers.

'Tomorrow,' she mumbled.

With the fire now burning brightly, the room had become quite warm, yet it would be tempting fate to remove her sweater. Perching on the edge of the sofa, she tried to will herself to be her usual calm self, the self she had been before they had started on this disastrous adventure. And he was hardly helping matters. Throwing herself moodily backwards, she overbalanced with a yell of alarm as the back of the sofa went down. Scrambling up, she stared at it in surprise just as Corbin rushed out, naked from the waist up.

'What the . . . Good lord, Verity, did you have to demolish the furniture?'

'Don't be stupid, it's meant to go down. It's a sofa bed.' Looking up, she found his face alight with laughter, and she was so astonished that she just gasped at him with her mouth open. He didn't even look like the same man. As she continued to stare, his smile slowly vanished.

'Half-naked men bother you, do they, Verity?' he asked softly, with a rather nasty gleam in his eyes.

'No, they do not,' she said shortly, recovering herself. 'Go and finish your wash!'

When he'd disappeared back into the bathroom, she transferred her blank gaze to the sofa. Well, at least it solved the problem of how they were to sleep. Firmly banishing the image of a laughing Corbin, she lay down on her back, legs straight, arms by her sides, then pulled the cover across her. She wasn't nervous, she told herself firmly. He wasn't likely to leap on her and demand sexual gratification. Of course he wasn't. He'd already intimated as much—besides, she didn't think he even liked her, let alone fancied her—not that she wanted him to, of course.

'All right to turn the light out?' he asked softly.

'Yes,' she said firmly. Not that it was pitch-black when he'd done so, for the fire gave the room a warm, orange glow that was quite adequate to see by. Certainly it showed her that Corbin still hadn't put his shirt and sweater back on. He'd also removed his socks, she discovered, as he climbed in beside her; his feet were cold.

'I can't sleep with socks on,' he murmured, and his voice sounded full of suppressed laughter.

'What a pity,' she muttered acidly. What did he find so damned funny?

'They'll soon warm up,' he soothed.

'Not on me, they won't. You stick to your own side of the bed, Corbin McCaid!'

'Certainly, the thought of doing anything else never even occurred to me.'

'Good. Goodnight,' she said with flat finality.

'Goodnight, Verity,' he said softly, promptly turning over on his side and dragging the cover with him.

Tugging it back with an impatient grunt, she turned over so that they were back to back.

'Back to back they faced each other, drew their

swords and shot each other,' he murmured irrepressibly, and Verity gave a reluctant laugh.

'Shut up, Corbin. Go to sleep.'

'I can't,' he said plaintively.

'Then count sheep!'

'One, two . . .'

'Corbin!'

'Sorry.'

CHAPTER THREE

HAVING told him to go to sleep, Verity now found she couldn't; the stupid buttons on the sofa kept digging into her back.

'Verity, will you stop fidgeting!' Corbin exclaimed.

'I can't get comfortable,' she muttered peevishly.

'Then turn over and cuddle my back—I don't damned well bite!'

'I didn't suppose you did,' she mumbled, doing as he suggested. Curving her thighs beneath his and putting one arm rather tentatively round his waist, she determinedly closed her eyes. She also determinedly closed her mind to the animal warmth and scent of him; those sort of problems she didn't need. It was just the unfamiliar feel of a man beside her, that was all it was, she tried to convince herself. Goodness knew, she shouldn't have had any trouble sleeping, she was tired to death! So why the devil did her mind persist in racing round and round when her body was dead? But slowly, as Corbin's breathing deepened, she drifted into sleep.

Sleepy grey-blue eyes were observing her closely

when she woke, and she blinked, startled. They didn't look in the least cold, she decided, not as they had before, a hundred years ago in the café in Paris. Then she wriggled in embarrassment when he made no attempt to look away.

'You're not totally unattractive when you're asleep,' he murmured.

'Oh, thank you very much! And will you please look away or get up or something, instead of looming over me?' she asked pettishly. 'It's very disconcerting.'

'And we mustn't disconcert Miss Lang, must we?' he asked softly. With a rather evil grin, he moved away to perch on the edge of the bed. 'I just thought you might like to know you looked like a baby panda.'

'Thank you,' she said tartly, knowing exactly what she must look like with the mascara she hadn't bothered to remove the night before smudging beneath her eyes. 'You don't exactly look like an advertisement for the man about town yourself.' And neither did he. On the other hand, he didn't look totally unattractive either. A stubbled chin and ruffled hair seemed to suit him. Despite his rumpled state, there was a sleepy warmth about him that she was horrified to find attracted her. If she raised her head just a fraction, she'd be able to kiss him—then wondered, mortified, if he'd read the invitation in her eyes, because his head slowly lowered towards her. Giving a hasty little shove at his chest, she rolled away, only to eye him warily as he laughed.

'No?' he queried lazily.

'No,' she said firmly, but was disgusted by the husky quality in her voice. 'You made the rules, remember? Kindly stick to them.'

'Ah, but that was before I'd seen you first thing in the morning,' he teased.

'Corbin!' she said, exasperated, hauling herself into a sitting position. 'Will you stop playing the fool? And I'd very much like to know why you're being so amiable, all of a sudden.'

'I've always been amiable, you've just never noticed.'

'Oh, funny,' she said in disgust. Shoving his legs to one side, she got up. It was still raining, she saw, the small latticed window was running with water, and she sighed. 'It seemed so very straightforward in Paris, didn't it? And now look at us. You behaving totally out of character.'

'How do you know it's out of character?' he asked with a lazy smile.

'What?' she asked, startled. 'Of course it's out of character! You were coolly remote, distant, and then bad-tempered . . .'

'Ah, but why, Verity?' he asked softly.

'What do you mean, why?' she asked irritably. 'Because that was—*is*—your nature, presumably. Even David said you were—er—difficult,' she hastily substituted, deciding she could hardly tell him what David had really said. They were supposed to be friends, after all.

'Only difficult?' he asked softly. 'That was

restrained of him. But yes, I suppose I am. I was also in a temper that day . . .'

'Oh, who would have guessed it?' she asked sarcastically, and unbelievably he laughed.

'Also, I was quite terrified of meeting the perfect Miss Lang.'

'That, I do believe,' she muttered.

'No, truly, I'd had this paragon held up to me, your virtues extolled until I was heartily sick of the sound of you.'

Yes, that sounded like David; complete overkill. 'He means well,' she murmured, 'but the day I believe you are terrified of anything is the day I believe the moon is made of cheese. If you can drive a lethal piece of machinery round a track at heaven knows how many miles an hour, meeting little old me must be a piece of cake!'

'No—there are no people in my lethal piece of machinery as you call it. Only me. Me, I can cope with. It's other people that cause the problems.'

'Do they? I don't think I believe that, either,' she remarked with a faint smile. Now that he was no longer looming over her, she found her equilibrium had returned, for which she was extremely thankful. Glancing at the smooth chest, the flat stomach, the fit, hard body, he didn't look as though he'd have trouble with anything.

'Do you miss it?' she asked, wanting to give his thoughts a new direction. 'Motor racing?'

'Miss it?' he exclaimed, and for a moment he sounded almost bitter. Staring at her as though he was assessing her, he suddenly shook his head. 'No,' he said flatly, and she wondered just what nerve she'd touched this time. 'You'd never heard of me, had you?' he asked slowly.

'No,' she admitted, and just as suddenly he relaxed again.

'No,' he echoed softly, then with a half-laugh he slapped her rump in a friendly fashion and got to his feet. 'We'd best go into town and have some breakfast. Then I'll ring the agent, and find out what the hell he's playing at.'

'OK. I'll clear away our things, tidy myself up,' she said equably, but her mind was filled with speculation. What had happened to make motor racing a taboo subject? David had hedged off when she'd asked—and now Corbin had done the same.

When they were ready, Corbin wearing a navy jumper which darkened his eyes, made them look bluer, they walked down to the harbour. The rain had eased off and was now only a light drizzle. Corbin carried the cases and Verity his golf clubs. Locking everything back in the car, they walked slowly towards the little bridge. There were no yachts bobbing at their anchors today, no tourists, the cafés and bars were all closed. The floating restaurant had canvas securely warped across it, hiding the interior from prying eyes. A strong wind whipped the surface of the racing river into white-caps as it thundered towards the bridge arches, and Verity gave a small shiver, pushing her hands more securely into the pockets of her sheepskin.

Auray itself seemed a hive of activity, and as they walked further into the town she saw why. The fish market was in progress, and they were forced to edge past the noisy throng on the other side of the road. Finding a café that did something more substantial than hot buttered croissants, they ate hungrily. Corbin used the café phone to call the agent, and Verity sat back with a sigh of contentment. Amazing how much better one felt with a full stomach.

'What did he say?' she asked, when Corbin returned to the table.

'He couldn't believe it. Said the house must have been vandalised.'

'It didn't look vandalised . . .'

'No, but that's the only explanation he could come up with. To be honest, he sounded totally incredulous. Admittedly, he hadn't inspected the house personally, or not recently. Anyway, he's ringing the local agent and will get him to meet us here.' Turning away, he ordered more coffee. 'We can't do much, I suppose, until the house is sorted out.'

'No,' she murmured absently as she stared out through the window. She enjoyed watching people. Young, old, hurrying about their business, or strolling unconcernedly from shop to shop. She loved France, especially Britanny; loved their dry humour, the way they wouldn't be hurried. 'Mind if I have a quick wander round while you're waiting?' she asked.

'A contradiction in terms,' he smiled, 'but no, you go ahead. While you're out, see if you can find a shop that sells computers, will you? I'll need one—or you will,' he added drily.

'Going to tell me why?' she asked softly.

'Didn't David tell you?'

'No, he said to ask you.'

'Oh, well, I'll tell you later. Go on, or you won't have time before the agent arrives.'

She found a shop that sold computers, even recognised one or two makes, and she supposed they were pretty much universal. They seemed more expensive than in England, but didn't really know if that was a problem. She had no idea how wealthy Corbin was, although she supposed vaguely that racing drivers earned a good fee. She didn't even know how much he was going to pay her, which seemed crazy. Fancy not asking!

When she returned to the café, a slim, fair-haired man was sitting talking to Corbin, and at her entrance they both got to their feet. The agent looked worried, as well he might, and with a brusque nod to Verity he led the way out and back to the harbour. Half-way down the steep cobbled hill he stopped, and Corbin and Verity nearly ran into his back—and she knew. Suddenly she knew. So did Corbin. Not wishing to dent his pride any further, she walked casually across the lane, as though her attention had been captured by something in the window of the antique shop. She watched their reflections in the glass in front of her, saw Corbin point across the river, saw the agent shake his head and she grinned. Well, it was an easy enough mistake to make, she thought. The directions Corbin had been given all depended on which way you approached Auray. They'd been told to go across the river, and so they had, unfortunately from the wrong direction. Also unfortunately, there were little cobbled lanes both sides of the river which were virtually identical . . .

'Verity!'

'Mm? Oh, coming.' Keeping her face carefully blank, she walked across to join them. 'Have we found somewhere else? Oh, this looks splendid,' she enthused. Ignoring Corbin's sour expression and the agent's astonishment, she whipped the key out of his hand and set off up the steps of the little ivy-covered house that seemed to huddle between its neighbours as though seeking warmth. It was set back a little way from the lane, so there was even enough room to park the car. Fitting the key in the brown front door, she pushed it wide—and a happy grin spread over her face. It was lovely. The hall was narrow, with a flight of stairs at the far end. To her left was a little room that would be ideal for Corbin's study. To the right, the lounge. Dining-room and kitchen were on opposite sides of the staircase. Running lightly upstairs, she pushed open doors. Three bedrooms, one with en-suite bathroom—Corbin's, she would bet, and a separate bathroom for the *hoi polloi*.

'It's perfect!' she exclaimed, descending the

stairs just as Corbin came in the front door. 'Absolutely perfect.'

'Good,' he muttered, hands thrust into his jacket pockets. Rocking backwards and forwards on the balls of his feet, he surveyed her moodily. 'You're a lousy actress, Verity Lang.'

Laughing, she stepped off the last stair and went to stand in front of him. 'But kind,' she murmured. 'Has Mr Superior gone?'

'Mm, firmly convinced that the English are even more stupid than he'd previously thought.'

'See if we care,' she teased with a wide grin. 'Still, it's odd that the key fitted all three doors, isn't it?' she queried. Then, pushing the thought aside, she added practically, 'Now, priorities are food, heating and bedding. Give me five minutes to hunt in the cupboards, see what we have, then I'll go shopping.' Turning away to go back to the kitchen, she called over her shoulder, 'I found a shop that sells computers, just up the road from the café.'

While Verity trundled round the supermarket, Corbin went to arrange for a computer to be delivered. Once she was organised, she could do her shopping once a week. It was after one o'clock when she'd bought all she needed, so she decided to have lunch out. Presumably Corbin would have the sense to do the same. By the time she'd finished, the shops were just closing for the afternoon and she wandered slowly back to the house, her shopping clasped in her arms.

Corbin's car was now parked outside, so presumably he'd unloaded their cases.

'Where the devil have you been?' he demanded as she pushed open the front door.

'You know where I've been,' she exclaimed in astonishment. 'I didn't expect you'd be back yet.'

'Well, I am,' he retorted disagreeably, and Verity sighed. So much for a change in his personality, although she might have known his denial of being anything but amiable wouldn't be entirely true. You didn't get to be world champion by being amiable.

'Sorry,' he sighed. 'It's just that someone's coming to install a phone, and I need to go out.'

'Well, I'm here now,' she soothed. 'What time is he coming?'

'I don't know. Some time this afternoon, he said. If they're anything like their English counterparts, it will be next month!' he added disagreeably. 'I'll see you later.'

'OK,' she said calmly. 'But I'd be extremely grateful if you didn't take your bad temper out on me.'

'I'm not——' he began. Then, pulling a face, he let his breath out on a long sigh. 'I'm not altogether sure I'm going to like you,' he muttered wryly. 'You're beginning to sound suspiciously like my mother. Did you get all the things we need?'

'Mm, I think so. I put everything on my credit card. I hope that's all right?'

'Sure, I'll settle it when the bill comes in. The

computer will be delivered some time next week; that will give us time to get into a routine.'

'Yes. I got lamb for dinner; it might be best to make a stew or something, then it won't matter if you're late.'

'I was expecting to be told to eat out—or at least asked where I was going. Never do the obvious, do you?'

'I don't know what the obvious is,' she said softly, a statement which seemed to startle him, for he stared at her in astonishment.

Widening her eyes at him, she gave a little smile and slowly, infinitely slowly, the harshness went out of his face and he gave a grunt of laughter. 'Infuriating girl,' he murmured. 'Oh, well, I'll see you later . . .'

When he'd gone, she put the lamb on to cook, then gave the bedrooms a good clean, made sure the beds were aired, then started on the kitchen. By the time Corbin returned just after seven, the telephone had been installed and the stew was bubbling on the stove.

'You look as though you've been busy.' She smiled, indicating the pile of exercise books and box of pencils he carried.

'Mm.' Sitting at the table, accepting the cup of coffee she handed him, he stared at her speculatively for a moment. 'Sit down, Verity.'

Obeying, she waited, and whatever she had been expecting it certainly wasn't to be told he was going to write a book.

'A book?' she asked blankly.

'Don't you think I'm capable?' he asked a trifle stiffly, and she thought, oh, lord, now I've hurt his feelings.

'I have no idea whether you're capable or not,' she said carefully. 'It was just that your statement was rather unexpected. David made it sound as though you were a Soviet spy at the very least.'

'David would,' he agreed, relaxing slightly. Leaning his elbows on the table, he stared at her seriously for a moment. 'No one is to know, Verity. *No one,*' he emphasised. 'Only three people know: the publisher who commissioned it, David, and now you. David said you were discreet—that was partly why I agreed to hire you.'

'And the other reason?' she probed.

'He said you were unobtrusive.' He gave a little snort of laughter.

'I am, usually,' she asserted with a lame smile. 'And will be from now on,' she promised. 'We got off to a bad start, I think.'

'Mm. Which was naturally my fault,' he said, and she smiled warmly at the teasing light in his really rather nice eyes.

'I won't breathe a word,' she said as she got to her feet. 'I'm not a tittle-tattle. It will remain between the two of us.'

'Thank you.' Then, with the crooked little grin that gave his face quite extraordinary charm, he teased, 'Aren't you going to ask me what it's about?'

'What's it about?'

Laughing, he explained, 'Motor racing.'

'I'd never have guessed.' She ducked as he threw the salt pot at her.

When they'd eaten, Corbin stretched and gave a long, satisfied sigh. 'Thank you. You're a very good cook.'

'We aim to please,' she replied softly. Clearing the table, she loaded the sink and ran hot water into it. When he didn't move, she looked at him over her shoulder. 'Don't feel you have to entertain me, will you?'

'I wouldn't dream of it,' he countered smoothly, and she laughed. 'Although now that you've mentioned it, I suppose we ought to lay down some ground rules.'

'It might be wise,' she smiled.

'I've never had a housekeeper, so I'm not sure of the procedure, but I shan't expect you to remain in your room when you're not working. The lounge looks pretty comfortable. If I don't want your company, I can always stay in my study.'

'True.'

Getting to his feet, he wandered out. 'Oh, and Verity,' he went on, a gleam of amusement in his eyes as he put his back round the door, 'once I'm sorted out, I don't want to be disturbed—for any reason. Not meals, or calls. If you can leave something for me in the kitchen so that I can help myself when I get hungry, that will be fine. Likewise coffee. Apart from that, you have a free hand. If you have any problems, leave me a note. I shan't be ready for you to type anything for a while—and if my mother rings, I'm always out.'

'Fine,' she said with a wry smile.

The first few days passed swiftly, as Verity got to know the house and devised ways of cleaning without disturbing him. Not that she saw much of him; she didn't. He seemed to spend almost all his time shut away in the study. She made meals that could be heated quickly if he got hungry. There was always a pot of soup on the stove, always crusty bread, so if she was out shopping or whatever, he could help himself. Which he usually did, she was amused to notice, and had a mental picture of him sneaking out to the kitchen the moment her back was turned. When they met, he would vaguely smile, or not, depending on his mood. Sometimes he didn't even see her at all, she admitted with a grin. Once or twice he had passed her in the hall and seemed totally oblivious to her presence.

At the end of the first week he actually sought her out; he walked into the kitchen where she was preparing lunch for herself. His dark hair was tousled, as though he had been running his fingers through it, and there was a rather abstracted expression on his face.

'Verity?'

'Mm?'

'You've been here a week now, right?' he observed, as though she couldn't possibly have been able to keep track of the days—or he couldn't.

'Right,' she agreed solemnly.

'And—well, we've been getting on quite well, haven't we?' he asked, sounding rather more hopeful than expectant that she would agree.

'Certainly we have,' she agreed, straight-faced.

'So—well, I've decided you can stay.'

'Oh, thank you,' she said weakly, a little smile tugging at her mouth. As she continued to stare at him, her brown eyes full of spurious innocence, he burst out laughing.

'I have rather dumped things on you, haven't I?' he asked wryly.

'Which was made perfectly clear when I was asked to do the job,' she pointed out. 'Besides, the only real problem is your mother. She rings at least twice a day. I'm running out of excuses.'

'Oh, hell. I'll ring her tomorrow.'

'Promise?' she asked, with no expectation of him doing any such thing. She wasn't disappointed, and his air of helpless inadequacy only made her laugh. 'She sounds very nice,' she probed.

'She is very nice,' he admitted. 'Just persistent.'

Shaking her head at him, she asked, 'How's the book coming along?'

'Not too bad.' With a grin, he added with a rather touching little-boy innocence, 'Quite well, in fact.'

When she didn't comment, he gave a humorous little pout. 'You're not playing the game, Verity.

You're supposed to ask me about the characters, the plot . . .'

'Tell me about the plot,' she asked obediently, a teasing glint in her eyes.

'Verity! What a wretched girl you are!'

'I know. Horrendous. It's because you're such a terrible fellow.'

'I thought I'd been very good. I haven't been in a temper once this week.'

'No,' she agreed. 'Amazing, isn't it? So go on, tell me about it,' she prompted.

'It's a bit complicated . . .' He grinned when she snorted with disgust. 'Actually, I was sort of leading up to asking you a favour.'

'Ah.'

'Don't do that!' he exclaimed. 'You make me feel very obvious.'

'No, not obvious,' she comforted. 'What was it you wanted?'

'Well, I know you can drive, but I need to know how well,' he said, surprising her by the seeming *non sequitur*.

'How well do I need to drive?' she parried.

'I walked right into that one, didn't I?' he exclaimed. 'You really are the most exasperating girl.'

'Why? It's a reasonable question. Do I need to simply cope with the local traffic? Drive to Paris? England? Take part in a Grand Prix? What?'

'Close,' he admitted ruefully. 'Rally. Well, not exactly drive in one. I need to know how much instruction a woman would need before taking part in one. For the purposes of my book, of course.'

'Of course,' she acceded drily. 'And does a woman need more instruction than a man?' she asked sweetly.

'I don't know.' He frowned, quite missing the point. 'Would you think so?'

'No, Corbin, I wouldn't!' She laughed. 'And why me?'

'Well, to be honest, I couldn't find anyone else. Not at short notice, anyway.' He laughed openly at her look of disgust. 'So will you? Only for a day.'

'Where? And what in? Surely not in your precious Merc.'

'Don't be silly! My car wouldn't be any good at all. No, I've arranged to borrow a car; we can practise in the forest near Erdeven. Lord knows, there's enough of it.'

'Don't we need permission?'

'No, of course we don't! They're only farm tracks!'

'Oh, well, of course, they're quite unimportant,' she agreed solemnly. 'I'm sure the farmers won't mind at all.'

'Verity! I could smack you sometimes.' Then, changing the subject, and walking across to the stove, he peered hopefully into the saucepan. 'What's for lunch? I'm starving.'

While they were eating, he explained all about the computer that was being delivered the next day,

just as though she'd never even heard of one, let
alone used one. 'It will be much easier, you
know. If you type up my notes into it, I can then
edit and alter to my heart's content. I had a
demonstration in Vannes. In fact, seeing as
you're so busy in the house, I might just learn to
do my own typing.'

'I'm sure you'll cope beautifully,' she said,
straight-faced. Having seen the performance he
made when the lights had fused, she had strong
doubts about his ability to use a computer.
However, time would tell.

He dragged her off to the forest at almost the
crack of dawn the next morning, and it said much
for her easy disposition that she didn't grumble
once. It was a damp, chilly morning, the ground
mist not yet dispersed, but as they drove into the
yard of the little garage in Ploermel to collect the
rally car Verity began to have second thoughts. It
looked a very professional piece of machinery,
and probably expensive. Suppose she crashed it?
Could one get insurance for rally cars?

'Come on, Verity,' he said impatiently,
tugging open her door. 'Let's get started.'

Climbing out, she followed him across to the
other vehicle. Nodding at the mechanic, who was
looking as dubious as she felt, she climbed awkwardly into the passenger seat. Taking the helmet
he handed her and balancing it on her lap, her
doubts increased. How fast was he expecting her
to drive, for goodness' sake? Although she was a
competent driver, the roads she normally used

had hardly prepared her for speed races.

'Are you quite sure this is a good idea?' she asked hesitantly. 'Suppose we have an accident?'

'Don't be so chicken-hearted, Verity. I expected better of you.'

'Did you, indeed?' she remarked as he drove out of the yard.

Driving across the main road, he steered into the forest and, after a few minutes of following the rutted track, pulled up in a small clearing. 'OK, Verity, let's change places.'

Climbing out reluctantly, she took her place behind the wheel, then, staring rather dubiously at the helmet, plonked it on her head.

'Do it up,' he instructed, buckling his own helmet into place. When she'd done so, he continued, 'Now the seat-belt. Right. Gears much as you find in an ordinary car, a bit more positive maybe, and the steering's power-assisted, so don't over-correct. You drive much as you normally do, only a bit faster. Don't stamp on the brake, otherwise we'll fishtail and end up in the trees—in fact, use the gears rather than the brake, and always accelerate out of corners positively. All right?'

'Fine,' she said weakly.

'Right, off you go. I'll alert you to corners, hazards and so on. Just follow my instructions.'

At first, she drove slowly to get the feel of the car, ignoring his tuts and exhortations to go faster. She absolutely refused to be panicked into making a mistake.

'Verity,' he complained, 'it's not an old people's outing.'

'No, it isn't, and if you don't keep quiet and let me do this my way, neither of us will grow old enough to ever go on an old people's outing!' she threatened.

When she felt confident enough to increase her speed, she took a deep breath and eased her foot down, murmuring, 'Right, now let's try.'

As Corbin talked her through it, she concentrated on the track. Ignoring the trees flashing past, her mouth set in a determined line, she grimly followed his instructions.

'Accelerate out!' he yelled above the noise of the engine as she let the speed fall off. 'You should be in fourth!'

'I should be at home,' she grumbled rebelliously. Whatever she did, it always seemed to be wrong; and, as she should have known, Corbin was not the most patient of instructors.

After an hour of being shouted at, and groans of theatrical despair and sarcasm, her arms trembling with the effort to hold the bucking car on the track, she took the next corner too fast. Frantically braking, she caused the very thing Corbin had warned her about; the rear of the car fishtailed into the ditch. As the engine stalled, she switched it off.

'I told you . . .' he began furiously.

'Don't say it,' she warned, turning to glare at him. 'Just don't say it.'

'Well, honestly, Verity,' he retorted in disgust.

'A rank amateur would have had more sense.'

'I *am* a rank amateur!' she yelled. Wrenching off her helmet, she took a deep, steadying breath before running her fingers through her flattened hair. 'So now you know,' she said sulkily. 'Women need more than a couple of hours' instruction before they become rally drivers!'

She was aware of him removing his own helmet and turning to face her as she stared grimly through the windscreen. And if he said one more word on the subject, she thought mutinously, she'd hit him!

'I did say a day, if you remember,' he said quietly, putting out a gentle hand and turning her face towards him. 'Actually,' he added, his mouth pulled into a grin, 'you did very well.'

'Very well?' she asked, astonished. 'You've been moaning and complaining ever since we started!'

'Only to keep you on your toes,' he admitted outrageously.

'On my toes?' she spluttered. 'I'll give you toes, you . . .'

Holding up his hands, he cried, *'Pax?'* And as she slowly relaxed he grinned. 'Want to drive us back to the yard?'

'You mean you actually trust me to get us that far?'

'Stop griping,' he laughed. 'Come on, put your hat back on.'

Doing as he said with marked reluctance, she put the car in neutral before switching on the engine. 'Always supposing I can get it out of the ditch, that is,' she muttered.

'You will, it has four-wheel drive,' he soothed as he refastened his seat-belt.

Giving a humph, she put it in first and, balancing the power between accelerator and clutch, slowly let off the handbrake. Feeling the wheels grip, she cautiously drove back on to the track and headed back the way they'd come. It wasn't so much that she was furious with him, but with herself; she had expected to do a lot better. Chewing the inside of her lip, she suddenly brought the car to a halt. Turning to face him, she said a little defiantly, 'Can I have another go? On the way back?' and knew by his smile that he had expected her to do just that. Slapping his arm, she turned back to stare through the windscreen.

'Go!' he suddenly shouted, and Verity shot forward with enough force to throw them both backwards. Grimly concentrating on everything he had told her, using the gears instead of the brake, accelerating smoothly out of corners, they slithered and rocked back to the clearing. With a big sigh, she switched off the engine and leaned limply back.

'Phew.' Removing her helmet with hands that shook, she turned to face him. Raising her eyebrows, she waited for his comments.

'Not bad, not bad at all—considering.'

'Considering what?' she asked, incensed. 'Considering I'm a woman?'

'No—o,' he drawled infuriatingly slowly, 'considering the very limited instruction.' He laughed at her astonishment. 'You did very well; excellently, in fact. Truly. If ever I need a co-driver, I'll know where to look.'

'Do you drive in rallies?' she asked, surprised.

'Mm, once the season ends, I usually co-drive for Peter Ford, or have been for the past three years . . .' Suddenly he looked sad again, haunted.

'Corbin?' she probed gently.

Shaking his head, as if to rid it of odd notions, he smiled. 'Want to drive back to the yard?'

'No, you do it, I'm exhausted,' she confessed with a rueful smile. 'Women's lib just collapsed in on itself.' Unbuckling her seat-belt, she climbed out and stretched her aching back. Taking deep breaths to dispel her tension, she stared up at the tall pine trees. Forests always seemed to make her feel claustrophobic, maybe because she couldn't see the sky. It was quiet, too—she couldn't even hear any birds—and she jumped as Corbin put warm palms on her shoulders.

'Nervous?' he asked, sounding surprised. 'I was beginning to think nothing daunted the competent Miss Lang.'

Turning her head, she gave him a faint smile. 'I was just thinking how quiet it was.'

'And isolated?' he asked gently. 'Afraid I'll suddenly turn into a ravening beast?'

'Heavens, no!' she exclaimed. 'That was the last thing I'd expect——' She broke off as her attention was diverted. Standing on tiptoe, she peered into his eyes, then laughed delightedly. 'They're green! Your eyes,' she explained when he looked puzzled. 'They take on whatever colour you wear.' And she pinched the material of his green anorak between finger and thumb for emphasis.

'Yes,' he murmured, clearly embarrassed, and she gave a faint smile. For a confident man, he always seemed awkward when talking about himself.

'Better not wear yellow or pink, then,' she teased. Moving away, she climbed into the passenger seat of the car.

When they arrived back at the house, a delivery van was parked ostentatiously outside, and Corbin gave an exclamation of delight. 'Hey, the computer's arrived.'

Scrambling boyishly out of the car, he strode up to the driver, who was waiting impatiently on the cobbles. Shaking her head and grinning at his enthusiasm, Verity followed more slowly. What a mass of contradictions the man was!

Leaving him to play with his new toy, she went to wash and change before beginning on the lunch. Not that there was much chance of Corbin actually leaving his new plaything to come and eat, she thought ruefully. No doubt she wouldn't see him for days—or at least a couple of hours, she amended humorously as she heard him yell for her.

'Verity!'

With a little sigh, she wiped the flour from her hands and walked along to the study. Pushing open the door, she stood framed in the entrance, watching him. The instruction book was lying, pages crumpled, in the corner of the room where he had obviously hurled it.

'Do you know anything about computers?' he demanded, all traces of his earlier good humour gone.

'A little,' she admitted. 'What seems to be the trouble?'

'It doesn't work!'

Walking across to the desk, she stared down at the screen. 'What is it you want to do?'

'I want to use it,' he muttered sarcastically. 'What the hell do you think I want to do? Eat it?'

'Corbin,' she said patiently, 'just tell me what you can't get it to do that you want it to do.'

Taking a deep breath, he stared at her from the corner of his eyes, then gave a shamefaced grin. 'Sorry. I don't know why you put up with me.'

'Neither do I,' she said drily. 'Go on.'

'I typed a few pages, just to get the feel of it, then stored them. Or so I thought. When I called them back, I only had the first page. Goodness knows where the rest of it is.'

'Ah. What program are you using?'

'Program?'

'Yes, Corbin, program. Word processing? Computing? What?'

'Oh, word processing. But it won't . . .'

Holding her hand up to stop his indignant explanation, she sat down in front of the screen and swiftly punched in the buttons to take her into the file header so that she could see what he'd been using. Chewing her lip, she quickly went through the program, aware of Corbin coming to lean on the chair back behind her.

'What are you doing?' he asked curiously, peering over her shoulder so that his hair brushed her face.

'Checking your options,' she murmured absently. 'When you first began, did you create a file or use an existing one?'

When he didn't answer, she turned her head to look at him, only to find he was far closer than she'd thought. Her mouth grazed with unconscious provocation across his cheek. Feeling suddenly awkward and embarrassed, she mumbled, 'Well?'

'I don't know,' he muttered absently, and she gave him a quick look, only to find him gazing rather blankly at her.

'Corbin? Did you press C or E?'

'Oh, E. I should have pressed C, shouldn't I?' he added with a little grunt of laughter.

'Yes, you should,' she retorted, suddenly finding it very hard to concentrate. 'Do you want to save the page you've already written, or will you be able to write it again?'

'Will it be easier to scrap it?'

'I think so. I'm not very expert, but I do think it would be best to create a file from one already set out. Then at least you'll know it will be right.'

'OK, start again. But will you tell me exactly what you're doing?'

'Right. We'll exit from this and go back to the manager screen.'

'The what?'

'The screen you start with when you put the disks in. It's called the manager screen.' Swiftly doing as she'd said, she then selected the manuscript template and proceeded to create a new file. 'Now, we need what?' she queried, turning to look up at him. 'Separate chapters?' And when he nodded she continued, 'OK, see where it says "mnscpts"? Well, that's a template already set up for you. Every time you want to create a new chapter, or begin something else, but still keep the same format, you put the cursor on that template and press C to create a new file. Clear so far?'

'Yes, teacher.'

Ignoring his soft sarcasm, she created the file, then explained quickly, 'This gives you double line spacing, margins of one and eight—do you want it justified?'

'Justified?' he asked blankly.

'Right and left margins the same, straight.'

'Oh, yes.'

'Right.' Swiftly making the alterations, she then asked, 'Is it to be a draft copy?'

'Yes.'

'Well, when you're ready to print, I'll show you how to alter that, but for the moment, it's all ready for you to type.'

Thankfully sliding from the chair, she indicated for him to take her place, yet he delayed for a moment. Eyeing her curiously, he asked, 'Where did you learn about computers?'

'You don't need to sound as though you think I don't have the brains to even know what one is,' she admonished. 'They gave us a crash course when I was doing hotel management. I'm no expert,' she warned. 'I just know how to get in and out of programs.'

'Oh. Quite a clever little thing, aren't you?'

'No. Just of average intelligence,' she said, more shortly than she'd intended. 'Go on, go and play. I'll leave your lunch to keep warm.' Giving him an odd, uncertain look, she went back to the kitchen.

Her face thoughtful, she began preparations for lunch. What on earth was the matter with her? She'd never reacted like that before. In all her dealings with the opposite sex, she'd always been confident, in control. It was all very perplexing. Deeming it not very wise to dwell on something she didn't understand—or didn't want to understand, she ruthlessly pushed it out of her mind.

After two days of barely seeing him, he emerged rather crumpled and tired-looking to stand in the kitchen doorway and watch as she stirred a large pot of soup.

Turning to smile at him, she asked, 'Hungry?'

'Starving.'

Swiftly cutting up the French loaf and putting the pieces into a basket, she put a pat of butter in a dish and transferred them to the pine kitchen table. Taking a large soup plate from the cupboard, she carefully ladled the hot, thick soup into it. Indicating he should sit, she placed it in front of him, then turned away to make the coffee.

'More?' she asked as he handed her the empty plate.

'Please. Aren't you eating?'

'I already have,' she said drily, glancing at the clock. 'Four-thirty in the afternoon is not my usual lunchtime.'

'No. Only mine,' he said ruefully. 'Sorry, is it very irritating?'

'No.' She smiled.

'Doesn't it really bother you?' he asked curiously.

'No, of course it doesn't. It's your choice. If you want to eat reheated food, then that's your problem, not mine,' she grinned.

Staring at her, his head on one side, he murmured, 'Nothing bothers Miss Lang—only Verity, is that it?'

'Something like that, I guess.' She wasn't sure if she was amused or cross that he persisted in making the distinction. She was all the same person.

'But not many things seem to bother you, do they?'

'No, not many,' she replied agreeably, then smiled when he pulled a face of disgust. But she had no intention of baring her soul to him, and if that was what he wanted then he'd just have to want.

'I'm going to have a shower and change, and then go out for some fresh air,' he remarked when he'd finished eating. 'Don't worry about dinner tonight, I'll eat out.'

'All right,' she said amiably. 'Did you make all those calls on the list?' she prompted, then smiled as he pulled a face. 'Your mother?' she asked without hope.

'I'll do it tomorrow,' he promised blithely.

'Except that tomorrow never comes,' she said softly, which made him grin.

CHAPTER FOUR

HE'D only been gone a few seconds when she heard the front door bell, then Corbin's hasty footsteps as he retreated.

'Answer it, will you, Verity?' he begged, erupting back into the kitchen.

'Yes,' she said on a long sigh. Really, the man was becoming positively paranoid. Who the hell was he expecting? The bailiffs?

It was a telegram, and Verity accepted it as though it might be a time-bomb. She didn't like telegrams, she always associated them with bad news. Quite why, she didn't know, because as far as she remembered she'd never received one in her life.

'Telegram for you,' she murmured, thrusting it at him as she returned to the kitchen, and Corbin too stared at it as though it might bite. Then, with an impatient sigh, he ripped it open.

'Oh, hell,' he muttered. 'It's from my mother; she's coming for a visit. Where the hell did she get the address from?'

'From directory enquiries, I shouldn't wonder . . .'

'No, she wouldn't,' he interrupted. 'They were instructed not to give out the address.' With a look of disgust, he crumpled the telegram and threw it on the table. 'That woman would make Sherlock Holmes look like the veriest amateur. Does she have to do these things to me?'

'You should have answered her telephone calls, then,' she said unsympathetically. 'When's she coming?'

'Tomorrow. Oh, hell.'

'Don't you like her?' she asked curiously.

'Of course I like her. Don't be so damned stupid, Verity!' Giving her a look of dislike, he muttered, 'I'm going out!'

Staring after him in bewilderment as he slammed out of the kitchen, she slowly walked across to the piece of crumpled paper and smoothed it out.

'Be with you Thursday. No good ringing me, am not at home. Love, Stella,' she read. Stella? Not Mother? Well, it should be interesting, she thought as she remembered David's rather caustic comments about Corbin's mother. But just exactly why did Corbin object to his mother coming? She somehow didn't think it was for the reasons David had put forward.

Corbin's burst of temper in the kitchen didn't seem to have abated when he returned. He wandered moodily into the lounge, glared at her and wandered out again, and she heard his study door slam. The next morning, he was even worse. Twitchy and bad-tempered until Verity became quite exasperated. Every time they encountered one another, he seemed to have a different complaint. First it was the doorbell, then the telephone—the voices of the market traders in the street that intruded into his thoughts, even the weather came in for its share. Well, there was nothing she could do about the street noises or the elements, but she could do something about the phone and the doorbell. She could move them further along the hall where he wasn't so likely to hear them! Finding an electrician at short notice didn't seem to be a problem in France, and he was there within half an hour. It only took him a few minutes to extend the wire from the doorbell and put in a new socket for the telephone. Rather pleased with her resourcefulness, she was quite unprepared for Corbin's further burst of temper.

'It's like living in a damned morgue!' he grumbled late that afternoon when he came into the kitchen where she was ironing. 'Where the devil have you been?'

'I haven't been anywhere,' she exclaimed, surprised.

'Yes, you have! I couldn't find you.'

'Corbin, you were the one who told me to be silent!'

'There's silent and silent,' he retorted crossly. 'I don't hear the phone, the doorbell, the hoover, anything! And why haven't I had any messages?'

'Because there haven't been any,' she said crossly. 'Honestly, Corbin, you sound like a petulant schoolboy.'

'Don't be so damned rude! And may I remind you I am your employer—not someone to be treated as though I were retarded!'

Opening her mouth to give a spirited retort, she suddenly saw how ridiculous they were being. Her mouth curving into a wry smile, she murmured softly, ' "Humoured" is the word. Want me to leave?'

'No!' he exclaimed. Letting his breath out in a soft explosion, he ran his hands through his tangled hair, then gave her a rather sheepish grin. 'Petulant?' he queried wryly.

'Mm hm.'

Giving a little snort of laughter, he leaned his broad shoulders against the doorframe, arms folded across his chest. 'I'm sorry,' he apologised, 'I always get like this when a visit from my mother is imminent. I thought she'd be here by now,' he grumbled moodily. 'Why can't she be like normal people and tell you what time she's arriving? It's like living with a time-bomb.'

'Oh, I couldn't agree more,' she agreed softly, and he had the grace to look ashamed.

'Sorry, Verity. You know what'll happen, don't you? We'll just get to the point when we think she's not coming after all, when she'll arrive and set us all at sixes and sevens.'

'Well, the time won't go any faster with you ranging around, Corbin. Why don't you go and do some work on your book?'

'I'm not in the mood,' he mumbled. Then, chewing his lip with an uncharacteristic gesture of hesitance, he murmured, 'Verity?'

'Mm?'

'My mother's a bit—well, she's a bit—— Oh, hell, different. I suppose one could say intrusive. She might—er—ask you embarrassing questions.' Walking across the kitchen, he leaned against the work surface and began fiddling with the pepper mill. His movements and manner oddly uncertain, he murmured again, 'Verity?'

'Yes?' she answered, amused. Corbin betraying nervousness was intriguing to say the least.

'Did David say anything about her?'

'Not much, except that she had a disconcerting habit of producing strange females for your inspection—although quite how she managed that when she can never find you, I'm not sure.'

Giving her an absent smile, he suddenly put the pepper mill down with an abrupt movement and turned decisively towards her. 'Verity?'

'Yes, Corbin.'

'When she comes, I need—well, I need to give the impression that you and I are . . .'

'Romantically involved?' she asked helpfully.

'Yes!' he said, sounding fervently thankful that he didn't have to put it into words. Then, after staring at her silently for a few seconds, he muttered, 'I suppose you want to know why.'

'No. You don't have to give me a reason,' she said softly, and was glad she had let him off the hook when he looked inordinately relieved.

'But you will do it?' he asked hopefully, and

when she didn't immediately answer he burst out, 'Dammit, Verity, I'm only trying to find out if you think it will harm your reputation! She's the most inveterate gossip. She'll tell all and sundry.'

'But I don't know all and sundry,' she responded, amused.

'You will when Stella gets going,' he mumbled. 'She'll probably invite everybody here. Even the fact that she doesn't speak a word of French won't stop her telling everyone she meets in Auray. So will it harm your reputation? David said you were a very private person, and—well, it didn't seem to matter then, I didn't know you . . .'

'And when you met me, you didn't like me?'

'Mm, something like that,' he said wryly.

Giving him a teasing smile, she said gently, 'Surely people thinking I'm your mistress can only enhance my reputation? Can't it?'

'Can it?' he asked blankly.

'Of course. Think of the speculation! "What does the so-very-ordinary Miss Lang have that would attract the devastating Corbin McCaid?" No, no, I assure you, my reputation will be made.'

'Verity! Stop being facetious. Devastating?' he asked with a little grin.

Laughing and refusing to answer, she denied, 'I wasn't being facetious. I meant it. The gentlemen hereabouts will view me with a hitherto unknown interest—and naturally come to only one conclusion.'

'They will?' he asked, his expression one of avid fascination. Although she did note that his rather nice mouth gave just the suspicion of a twitch.

'Mm.'

'Well, what?' he asked exasperated.

'Why, that I must be terrific in bed, of course.'

'Verity!'

'What?' she asked innocently. 'Don't tell me I've shocked you, Corbin. That I won't believe.'

'Then you should. Because you have,' he said drily. 'For someone so quiet and gentle-looking, you're full of surprises, aren't you? First sarcastic, then bad-tempered, then coping quietly and serenely with my moods! What else is hidden in that slim frame, I wonder?'

'Do you?' she asked, one eyebrow raised.

'Yes. Do you really not mind people thinking that of you?'

'No. Why should I?'

'I really don't know,' he confessed, looking as bemused as he sounded. 'What an extraordinary girl you are. When I first saw you, I imagined you led a sheltered and quiet life, sitting at home each evening, knitting, embroidering . . .'

'Was this before or after you thought me an irritating burr in your side?' she broke in with soft interest.

'After,' he admitted, grinning at her.

'And now?'

'Well, now—now I'm just thoroughly intrigued.'

'There's no need to be,' she said mildly. 'I'm just an ordinary, hard-working, practical girl. And unobtrusive, of course,' she added, tongue in cheek. 'And you don't need to be concerned that I'll carry the romantic charade beyond what you want, if that's what's troubling you.'

'It isn't. To be honest, that never even occurred to me.'

'Then it should have done,' she reproved.

'Why? You have no desire to be my mistress. No desire to even be kissed by me. You said so—didn't you?' he asked softly.

'Mm, so I did,' she agreed, refusing to be drawn. 'You took me by surprise.'

'Does that mean you might be more amenable next time?' he asked interestedly.

'No, Corbin, it does not!' she said hastily, repressing the funny little shudder that went through her.

'So sure, Verity?'

'So sure,' she confirmed, which of course was a complete and utter lie. She wasn't sure at all. That was the trouble. Before he could resume his teasing, she said briskly, 'Now, back to practicalities. Does your mother have any violent likes and dislikes?'

'Don't think so,' he murmured without interest as he continued to observe her closely.

Picking up one of his shirts from the laundry basket at her feet, she determinedly turned her attention to ironing the collar. She didn't think she quite liked the way he was watching her.

'Have you ever been in love, Verity?' he asked softly.

'No,' she said calmly, turning the shirt and beginning on the sleeve.

'No?' he exclaimed in astonishment. Leaning more comfortably against the sink unit and folding his arms across his chest, he asked with suspicious mildness, 'Are you still a virgin?'

'Yes,' she confirmed with an inward smile. 'And you can take that speculative gleam out of your eye, Corbin McCaid. It's entirely by choice, I assure you. I'm quite happy with the status quo.'

'It doesn't bother you?'

'No, it doesn't. Why should it?'

'I don't know, except that most women I've ever met seem more than anxious to be rid of it.'

'Well, not me,' she said firmly, beginning on the other sleeve.

'You're not . . .?'

'No, Corbin, I'm not,' she said, her lips twitching.

'Extraordinary.'

'What's so extraordinary about it?' she asked, amused. 'If I meet someone I want to take it, then it will go. If I don't, it won't. Quite simple. If I never meet anyone who I think right for me, then no doubt I shall remain *virgo intacta,* as they say. Which airport will your mother come in to, do you think?' she asked, deliberately changing the subject.

'I've no idea. It depends which broomstick

she's using.'

Giving a snort of laughter, Verity returned her attention to her ironing. After a few minutes, he turned and went out.

Smiling widely, she finished ironing his shirt. It was true, it didn't particularly bother her. Oh, sometimes she wondered if maybe there was something wrong with her. Something in her make-up that prevented her from falling in love. Sometimes she even wondered what it would be like to be made love to, imagined how it would be. But the simple truth was, she'd never met anyone who made her feel special, made her feel that he was the one. Maybe she was too cautious, or maybe she was incapable of great emotion, but whatever the reason, if in fact there was one, none of them were matters she dwelt on with any degree of anguish. Her life was full and enjoyable at present. Maybe when she was thirty or forty those thoughts would be become more pronounced, hold more importance, but at the moment she was quite content. Certainly she didn't feel that she was missing something. So quite why Corbin's teasing about kissing her remained in her mind, she didn't know. Then she had her attention successfully diverted by the strident ring of the doorbell.

'She's here!' he hissed, rushing into the kitchen.

'Well, hadn't you better go and let her in?' she asked in amused exasperation.

'You go,' he murmured. 'No, wait,' he exclaimed, grabbing her arm, 'take your apron off first. I don't want her to think you're the . . .'

'Domestic?' she asked helpfully with a tinge of sarcasm. 'Home help?'

'Yes. No. Oh, I don't know. Oh, hell,' he muttered as the doorbell pealed again, 'go and answer it before she alerts the whole neighbourhood. She's quite likely to go knocking on people's doors, demanding to know where I am.'

Shaking her head at him, she carefully unplugged the iron before going out and along the hall. If she'd had a mental image of his mother at all, it would have been of a tall, rather regal, commanding figure. The woman standing on the top step looked as though she'd just gone ten rounds with a Sumo wrestler. Her hat was tilted drunkenly over one eye, her coat was unbuttoned, and she was short and dumpy.

'Ah! At last!' she exclaimed. 'I was beginning to think you were both going to ignore me. I knew you were in, you know. I could hear the radio playing.'

'Yes, well——' Verity began, only to find that she was talking to herself. Mrs McCaid had slipped past her, no doubt with the skill born of long practice, and advanced upon a sheepish-looking Corbin.

'I'm very cross with you,' she told him in ringing tones. 'You lied to me.'

'I did no such thing?' he exclaimed.

'Yes, you did. By omission, anyway. If I

hadn't collared David, I wouldn't have known about Verity. I wouldn't have know where you were in France, either!'

'I was going to write . . .' he began helplessly.

'Hah! And that's another lie! And not only do you lie to me, you make poor Verity lie to me, too! Not in! I bet you were standing beside her every time I phoned, mouthing at her to lie.'

'I was not, I . . .'

'Well, don't just stand there like a landed fish, Corbin. Give me a kiss?' she said with a complete about-face.

Rolling his eyes upwards and giving a long sigh, he picked his mother bodily off the floor and kissed her. 'There! Better?'

'Yes,' she murmured with a fond smile. 'Now, introduce me to Verity.' Turning swiftly for one so small and dumpy-looking, she stared at Verity with twinkling blue eyes. 'You're not at all . . .' she began, only to be hastily interrupted by Corbin.

'Mother!' he warned.

'I was only going to say, she wasn't at all like she sounded on the phone.'

'People never are, are they?' Verity asked, amused.

'No, do you know I got the shock of my life when I met George Dickens—you remember George, don't you, Corbin?' But, without waiting for Corbin to confirm or deny any knowledge of the said George, she hurried on, 'He always sounded tall! And quite incredibly good-looking. He was short and fat, and as bald as a coot! Do I sound tall?' she demanded of Verity.

'Taller,' she began, 'and—er——'

'Slimmer? Yes, I know. I really must go on a diet!' As they all heard frantic hooting from outside, Mrs McCaid cried, 'Oh, heavens, the taxi. Corbin, be a dear and pay him, I don't seem to have any French money on me—and get my luggage!' she yelled after him. Before Corbin was even out of the front door, she had linked her arm in Verity's and persuaded, 'Tea? I yearn for a cup of tea.'

'Would you prefer to sit in the lounge, or join me in the kitchen?'

'Well, I can hardly talk to you from the lounge if you're somewhere else, now can I? Kitchen, dear. Please don't think I have to be pampered.' As they walked into the kitchen, she added in a stage whisper, 'What I was really going to say is that you don't look the sort of girl I always imagined could rep—Corbin would fall in love with,' she hastily amended, giving Verity a look which clearly said, Don't you dare ask me what I was going to say.

'What did you imagine she would look like?' Verity asked gently, entering into the spirit of the thing. 'Glamorous?'

'Oh, dear me, no! Not glamorous! He wouldn't fall for that trick twice. No, plain. I thought you would be plain and homely.'

'I am,' she said, laughing.

'No, you aren't,' said Stella seriously, her brow furrowed. 'I thought so at first, when you opened the door—but you're not. You have a mobile face, always changing. And laughing eyes. Ah,' she sighed, 'what a sucker I am for laughing eyes. Corbin's father had laughing eyes. I miss him, you know.'

'How long is it since . . .?'

'Ten years. Sometimes it seems like forever —sometimes only yesterday . . .' Then she turned and beamed at Corbin as he came in, looking quite terrified that he might have left them alone too long. Was he afraid his mother would tell her something he didn't want her to know? It was beginning to seem like it, especially after his mother's hastily amended statement.

When Verity had made the tea, they sat at the kitchen table drinking it, the conversation idle and innocuous, yet she knew very well that Corbin couldn't wait to separate them. Every time he attempted to prise his mother away and take her up to her room, Mrs McCaid found yet another reason not to go. Verity found the whole thing quite hilarious.

When he eventually did manage to get his mother upstairs, Verity began preparations for dinner. After a great deal of thought, she'd decided on asparagus with lemon butter sauce for starters; it was light and easy to do and most people liked asparagus. It would be followed by veal medallions with artichoke bottoms and a selection of fresh vegetables. Corbin had told her not to go to any trouble, but she felt she could hardly do egg on toast, or even meat and two veg. His mother might pretend she didn't expect to be fussed over, but she guessed most mothers would want it just the same. Especially a mother as devoted as Stella seemed to be—and Verity was supposed to be in love with her son, and presumably one day become a daughter-in-law. Although, now that she'd met Stella, she wasn't so enamoured of the idea of deceiving her—yet it was obviously important to Corbin. Anyway, she wanted the meal to be nice for her own sake. She had her pride, too. As soon as the meal was underway, she went upstairs to bath and change.

Slipping her feet into black high heels, she surveyed herself in the long mirror. The deceptively simple sage green wool dress that she had picked up in a sale in Vannes was beautifully cut and gave her curves that she wasn't altogether sure she had. It also, she hoped, gave the impression that, although she had made an effort, she hadn't gone out of her way to dress up. The slight curl in her hair had been given a bit of assistance from a heated brush, and with her face carefully made-up she looked quite unlike her normal self. Almost elegant, she thought, amused. The subtle use of eyeshadow and mascara made her brown eyes look enormous, blusher emphasised her cheekbones and a soft pink lipstick enhanced her mouth. The whole effect did not add up to stunning beauty, but at least she looked presentable, she thought with a deprecating grin. With a quick spray of Gianni Versace to throat and wrists, she was ready. Giving herself an approving little nod in the mirror, she collected her lipstick and went out. There were one or two little adjustments she needed to make to the bedrooms before she went down, if his mother was to believe the fiction they were enacting.

As she joined Corbin in the lounge, he almost did a double take. 'Verity,' he exclaimed warmly, 'you look lovely.'

'Thank you,' she murmured graciously. 'Lovely' was maybe a little extravagant, she thought with an inward smile as she accepted the glass of sherry he handed her, but it was a welcome compliment, none the less. 'You don't look so bad yourself,' she teased. He was dressed in grey trousers, white shirt and dark red V-necked cashmere sweater. The colour gave extra warmth to his tanned skin, and she stared curiously at his eyes to see what colour they became when he wore red. Dark grey, she decided. His hair seemed darker, too, and gleamed with health under the artificial light. He also appeared to be a little ill at ease, and kept fidgeting with the stem of his wineglass.

'Do you . . .?'

'Are you . . .?' they both began together. Laughing, Verity gestured for him to continue.

'I was only going to say, are you nervous about the pretence? Not that you look it,' he said wryly.

'No,' she smiled. 'Although I'm not altogether

happy about deceiving her.'

'No,' he sighed. 'But believe me, it was necessary. David didn't lie about the string of women. Very determined lady, my mother.'

'Yes, but rather sweet,' she ventured.

'Sweet?' he asked with a grimace. 'Wait till she starts her inquisition. You won't think she's sweet then.' Putting his glass down, he walked the few paces to stand in front of her. Tilting up her chin with one long finger, taking her completely by surprise, he dropped a gentle kiss on her mouth. 'I am grateful, Verity. It's—oh, I don't know. It's difficult to explain, but it is important to me that her visit goes smoothly.'

'It will,' she promised, a slight huskiness in her voice. A promise she meant to keep. For all his odd ways, she was becoming rather fond of him—in a sisterly sort of way, she assured herself.

'Battle stations,' he whispered as they heard his mother's footsteps on the stairs. 'Just be—well, you know, just be natural . . . Sorry,' he quickly apologised. 'I just didn't want it to be . . .'

'Obvious?'

'Mm. Thanks, Verity.'

'I hope you write all this down,' his mother said tartly from the doorway.

'What?' he asked, bewildered.

'All these instructions you keep giving everybody,' she murmured, straight-faced. 'Instructions to me not to tell Verity this or that, and it looked uncommonly as if you were doing the same to Verity. Was he?' she demanded with a grin.

'Of course.' Verity smiled and heard Corbin nearly choke behind her. 'Don't overdo the meat, you don't like soggy vegetables . . .'

'My dear girl, if he told you that, he doesn't know me very well at all! I eat anything!'

Laughing, Verity excused herself to check on the dinner.

The meal went smoothly; there was talk, laughter, anecdotes exchanged. Stella chattered and teased; she had a rather sharp wit that had Verity laughing helplessly. Corbin just looked worried, and every time she caught his eye he gave her a strained smile. After the meal, they returned to the lounge and Verity made a fresh pot of coffee.

'I can't remember the last time I enjoyed myself so much,' Stella sighed with a warm smile at Verity. 'You're a very good listener,' she added. 'A rarity these days. I hope you appreciate it, Corbin.'

'Oh, I do, I do,' he said slyly, knowing she was having a dig at him. She always accused him of never listening to a word she said.

'So how do you get on with this old grouch?' she asked Verity.

'Oh, we get on very well,' she replied, with a sideways glance at Corbin. 'He commands—I obey.' And his mother laughed.

'He's a Scot. That's what it is, Verity, all Scotsmen are chauvinists. Spoilt rotten, the lot of them.'

'Rather a sweeping statement,' Corbin reproved with a smile. 'I'm not at all chauvinistic, and I certainly don't recall that I was ever spoilt. In fact, I'm always most courteous and thoughtful. Aren't I, darling?'

Giving him an old-fashioned look, Verity refilled the coffee-cups.

'Does he snore?' Stella asked in an artless stage whisper. 'His father did. I think that, of all their rotten habits, snoring gets to me the most.' And when Verity only gave a small smile, she persisted. 'Well, does he?'

'I wouldn't know,' she said softly. 'My bedroom is across the landing from his.' This statement that was greeted with a shout of disbelieving laughter, which only increased when Corbin gave her a quizzical look of bewilderment. He couldn't have done it more perfectly if he'd been primed, because it gave exactly the impression Verity intended to give.

At twelve, Stella finally went up to bed, and Verity and Corbin exchanged a small smile of relief. Corbin, presumably because no controversial topics were raised, and Verity because the evening had gone smoothly.

'Why did you tell her we had separate rooms? I thought the whole idea was for her to think that we didn't.'

'She didn't,' she murmured with a smile. 'It's a

sad fact of life, but tell the truth and no one believes it. Tell a lie and it's instantly accepted. If I'd told her, or even hinted that we slept together, she would have become suspicious. This way, she believes it implicitly. Besides, I left a few little clues in your room. And mine.' She grinned.

'What clues?'

Getting to her feet, she crooked her finger at him, then led the way upstairs. With a querying look at him for permission to enter his room, she walked inside. The lipstick she had carefully rolled across his dresser so that it went behind his cuff-link box was now standing up straight in front of it.

'Did you stand it up?' she asked.

'No. I didn't even know it was there. Whose is it? Yours?'

'Of course, and the fact that it is now in a different position from the one I left it in is proof that your mother has been having a little look-see.'

'But why? Why would she bother to come into my room to check?' he asked in bewilderment.

'Corbin! Don't be naïve. Women are curious creatures. Had I been beautiful, sexy, whatever, she probably wouldn't have doubted it for a moment. But because I'm not—and although I think she doesn't entirely dislike me—she couldn't be altogether sure we were telling the truth. For some reason, it seems desperately important to her that you're—well, in love with me. So I left a little clue. She would think, I hope, that in my haste to clear out my belongings from your room before she arrived, I'd forgotten the lipstick.'

'But why would you clear your belongings out? She knows very well I know she wouldn't be shocked that we sleep together.'

'Corbin,' she muttered with a tinge of exasperation, 'that isn't the point. The point is convincing her that I am sleeping with you. If I'd left my nightie or something, she'd think it had been planted. Don't ask me how I know! I just do.'

'Good heavens, we don't stand a chance, do we? I don't think I've ever heard anything so devious in my entire life!'

'Well, you're the one who wanted her convinced,' she said a shade crossly.

'I know. But how did you know she'd check?'

'Because I did!'

'Well, would you go prying into someone else's bedroom?'

'No. But then, I'm not like other women. I don't suffer from avid curiosity, for one thing . . .'

'That's not the only thing?' he muttered, staring at her as though she'd suddenly grown two heads.

'I also . . .' she continued, beginning to wish she'd never started the explanation, 'forgot to retrieve my toothbrush. And,' she added, marching across to her bedroom, 'I arranged a few bits and pieces on the end of my bed, as though I'd just opened the door and hurled them in.' She'd also jumbled her make-up on the dressing-table as though she'd hastily scooped it up from his room and dropped it down here. 'It's called subtlety,' she muttered.

'No it isn't,' he denied. 'It's called deviousness!'

Giving him a look of disgust, she led the way out.

'And that will convince her?' he asked, astonished. 'We don't need to be caught kissing and cuddling in corners?'

'No.' Did he have to sound as though that would have been extremely distasteful? Then she wondered why it should matter. Suddenly feeling extremely tired, she murmured, 'I'll go and clear up downstairs, then I'm going to bed.' Turning away, she walked along the landing and downstairs. 'On the other hand,' she muttered somewhat waspishly, 'she maybe thinks I climbed into your bed when you weren't looking, and you couldn't be bothered to turf me out.'

'Verity, that's an awful thing to say!' he exclaimed, hurrying after her. 'You do undervalue yourself!'

'No, I don't,' she sighed. 'Why should she believe you're attracted to me? It's much more likely the other way round.'

'But that makes me sound like a crass schoolboy without control, or an animal.'

'No, it doesn't. I expect she'll think you're

WOW!

THE MOST GENEROUS
FREE OFFER EVER!

From the Harlequin Reader Service®

GET 4 FREE BOOKS WORTH $10.00

Affix peel-off stickers to reply card

4 FOUR FREE BOOKS 4

4 FOUR FREE BOOKS 4

PLUS A FREE VICTORIAN PICTURE FRAME

AND A FREE MYSTERY GIFT!

NO COST! NO OBLIGATION TO BUY!
NO PURCHASE NECESSARY!

Because you're a reader of Harlequin romances, the publishers would like you to accept four brand-new Harlequin Presents® novels, with their compliments. Accepting this offer places you under no obligation to purchase any books, ever!

ACCEPT FOUR BRAND-NEW

YOURS

We'd like to send you four free Harlequin novels, worth $10.00, to introduce you to the benefits of the Harlequin Reader Service®. We hope your free books will convince you to subscribe, but that's up to you. Accepting them places you under no obligation to buy anything, but we hope you'll want to continue your membership in the Reader Service.

So unless we hear from you, once a month we'll send you 6 additional Harlequin Presents® novels to read and enjoy. If you choose to keep them, you'll pay just $2.24* per volume— a saving of 26¢ off the cover price. There is no charge for shipping and handling. There are no hidden extras! And you may cancel at anytime, for any reason, just by sending us a note or a shipping statement marked "cancel." You can even return any shipment to us at our expense. Either way, the free books and gifts are yours to keep!

ALSO FREE!
VICTORIAN PICTURE FRAME

This lovely Victorian pewter-finish miniature is perfect for displaying a treasured photograph—and it's yours *absolutely free*—when you accept our no-risk offer.

Perfect for a treasured Photograph

Plus a FREE mystery Gift! follow instructions at right.

WE EVEN PROVIDE FREE POSTAGE!

It costs you *nothing* to send for your free books — we've paid the postage on the attached reply card. And we'll pick up the postage on your shipment of free books and gifts, and also on any subsequent shipments of books, should you choose to become a subscriber. Unlike many book clubs, we charge *nothing* for postage and handling!

maybe fond of me,' she added, wishing he'd drop the subject. They seemed to have talked it to death.

'Or that you're damned good in bed!' he muttered, sounding so cross that she stared at him in astonishment.

'Or that, of course,' she agreed tiredly.

CHAPTER FIVE

WHEN Verity got up next morning, there was a note from Corbin by the kettle. He'd gone to play golf, and he didn't know what time he'd be back. Because of last night? she wondered. Because of their conversation? She'd lain awake for ages, trying to fathom out his rather odd remarks, his anger.

'Morning, Verity,' Mrs McCaid mumbled, coming into the kitchen. She was wearing a blue fluffy dressing-gown that made her look rounder than ever. 'You look very sombre. Anything wrong?'

'Mm? No, no, I'm fine,' she lied, forcing a smile. 'Corbin's gone to play golf,' she explained, crumpling his note.

'Avoiding me, is he? Oh, well, it's no more than I expected.' Sitting at the kitchen table, she accepted the cup of tea Verity passed her. 'I don't mean to infuriate him, you know,' she said rather sadly, her eyes on her cup. 'Or maybe I do, I don't know. Even just to get a reaction, however negative, is a positive step, isn't it?' she asked, then smiled lamely. 'That's rather a contradiction in terms, but you know what I mean, don't you?'

'Yes, I know,' Verity said gently.

'I know I drive him insane, but it was only because I was so determined to make him forget that—that viper! I knew that the girls I brought to see him weren't his sort, not really, and they weren't meant to be. They were to simply be a diversion, to try and make him see what he was missing. I see her, you know,' she rambled on, and Verity thought she probably didn't need an audience at all, just needed to talk, get off her chest something that had been bottled up too long. 'Lording it over everybody,' she continued morosely. 'Gives me regal little nods—so infuriating. She was never right for him, you know, never even loved him, I don't think—just wanted to share in the glamour, the fame. Only what she didn't seem to realise was that, however glamorous it looked to everyone else, motor racing is a difficult and dangerous sport. It needed all his concentration. He couldn't forever be out at parties, drinking, socialising. Shallow and mercenary, that's what she was. A pretty face isn't everything, Verity. Strength of character is so much more important, and compassion, warmth.'

'Yes,' she agreed. Then, giving one of her gentle smiles, she said softly. 'I'm not altogether sure I know who we're talking about.'

'Eve,' Mrs McCaid said, suddenly looking as bewildered as Verity felt.

'Eve?'

'His wife. Oh, don't tell me he hasn't told you

about her! Oh, what a fool. How can he base a relationship on half-truths, evasions? Oh, Verity, I'm sorry. Well, I don't care,' she muttered aggressively, 'he didn't precisely say I wasn't to tell you, not about her, anyway—so I'm going to. If he doesn't like it, it's his own fault! They met at some Press party five years ago. She was some sort of PA to somebody or other. He was just beginning to make a name for himself, winning races; he'd just been taken on by the Cobra team—you do know about the Cobra team?' she demanded.

'Er—no,' Verity confessed. 'I know very little about motor racing.'

'Oh, well, I don't know very much either, to be honest, except that Cobra was owned by an ex racing driver. He'd designed these new cars that seemed to be taking the motor-racing world by storm. He asked Corbin to drive for him; there was a lot of publicity, and Corbin became the darling of the track,' she said somewhat disparagingly, then laughed. 'He hated it! The groupies, the silly little girls thinking they were in love with him.' And Verity smiled.

'Yes,' Stella murmured, echoing Verity's amusement, 'you can just see him, can't you, putting up with all that? But Cobra needed the publicity, needed sponsors—and—well, Corbin had to put up with the whole merry-go-round. That was when he met Eve. I still can't understand how a man who was always so sensible could fall in love with that predatory viper! But he did.' She sighed. 'Fell hook, line and sinker for blonde hair and green eyes. Only he was determined to succeed as a racing driver, and he sensibly put her out of his mind. Or I thought he had. Two years ago they met again, and after a whirlwind courtship they married—and then the rot began to set in. She was bored. Standing in the pits having her photograph taken was all very fine once or twice, but *forever*?' she exclaimed comically. 'Oh, no. Especially if it was wet and cold. Miss Madam had expected to be pampered. Well, Corbin didn't have time to pamper her, he wanted to be world champion, and you don't get to be that by missing practice or staying out late at night. Corbin can be very single-minded when he chooses.'

'Yes,' Verity agreed, having experienced some of Corbin's single-mindedness first-hand. 'I suppose he thought Eve would understand.'

'Yes! And that just goes to show how stupid men can be. I watched him get more and more miserable, torn between his love for her and his love of motor racing. Then the rumours started, she was seen with other men, usually other drivers, even his team mate, the Frenchman. Oh, Verity, it was a nightmare!' And Verity was horrified to see tears trickle slowly down the plump cheeks.

'Ah, don't!' she murmured, distressed. Getting to her feet, she hurried round the table and bent to put her arm round the small, dejected figure. 'Don't. He's fine now.'

'No, he isn't! Oh, he's over her, obviously, or he wouldn't be here with you—and you don't know how glad I am, Verity!' she said fiercely. 'I told her when I saw her in London. Told her he'd forgotten her, found someone else!' Verity's eyes widened in sudden understanding. That was why he wanted his mother to think he was involved with Verity. He expected his mother to tell Eve—which she had. Oh, Corbin, she thought sadly, yet she could hardly blame him for wanting to rescue his pride.

'I hate her!' Stella continued vehemently. 'Everything that happened was her fault. Everything! Even winning the world championship that he'd worked so hard for was ruined. Oh, they couldn't take it away from him, but they might just as well have done. I hate her, Verity, and if she hadn't divorced him, I think I would have killed her. She ruined his life!'

Quite thoroughly bewildered and confused, having not the faintest idea what Stella was talking about, she murmured inanely, 'But he's all right now . . .'

'Is he? Do you ever get over that, Verity? The accusations, the scandal? Why in heaven's name couldn't he have bloody died instead of going into a coma? Then we wouldn't have this hanging over our heads. If he comes out of it, remembers what happened, it will start all over again! And I can't bear it! So that's why I keep trying to divert him, keep intruding into his life! I won't let him become a recluse!' And then, as if she were only just aware of what she had said, she focused startled eyes on Verity's concerned face, then flushed guiltily.

'Oh, Verity, I'm sorry. Of course he won't become a recluse, he has you now. I was just trying to explain why I behaved as I did.'

'What man?' Verity asked quietly. 'What man is in a coma?'

'His team-mate, Veroni—— Oh, Verity!' she exclaimed, clapping a hand over her mouth. 'I promised him I wouldn't tell you.'

'Well, you haven't,' she said wryly. 'I haven't the faintest idea what you're talking about.'

'The crash,' sighed Stella. 'I was talking about the crash. If it had happened in France, they'd have called it a crime of passion—only it didn't. It happened in Germany—and the blasted Germans don't have any passion! Not that I've ever found, anyway. Bit like the English. Anybody with half a brain could see why he'd done it, and if it had been anyone else but Veroni everyone would have thought it an accident, but as it was—well . . .'

'Are you trying to tell me that Corbin deliberately caused another driver to crash his car?' she asked slowly, her face shocked.

'Yes,' agreed the other woman ruefully. 'Does it make a difference, Verity? To the way you feel about him?' she asked worriedly. 'I know he told me not to tell you, but—oh, Verity, I feel you have the right to know. If you love him, it won't make any difference, will it? I've been so

worried. But if Veroni comes out of the coma,
as they seem to think he will, and he remembers, there'll be a court case and everything.
Corbin will be charged with manslaughter at
the very least.'

Getting to her feet and walking back to her
seat opposite, Verity sat down and stared at
Stella. 'Are you telling me,' she began quietly,
'that Corbin, during a race, in temper and
jealousy, deliberately forced this Veroni off the
track because he was having an affair with his
wife? Is that what you're telling me?'

'Yes.'

'That he cold-bloodedly tried to murder
him?'

'Not cold-bloodedly . . . He would have been
in a temper. He has a terrible temper Verity,
he . . .'

'No,' Verity said flatly.

'What?'

'No,' she repeated. 'Corbin wouldn't do
that,' she added with quiet conviction. 'We
must hope that this Veroni does come out of
the coma, does regain his memory, because if
there were no witnesses, as I assume there
weren't, then he's the only one who could clear
Corbin's name.'

'But Verity . . .'

'No,' she said again. Getting to her feet, she
picked up the empty tea-cups. 'Why not go and
get dressed, Mrs McCaid? I'll make some fresh
tea.'

'Oh, Verity,' she said helplessly, 'you weren't there, you don't know what he was like then.'

'Did Corbin say he did it?' she asked with a hauteur quite foreign to her nature.

'Well, no—he didn't say anything. Even at the inquiry—not that I was there, but other people were, they told me—he didn't say a word. Just asked them if they believed he had done it, and when they said yes, he walked out. They suspended him, or took away his licence or whatever they do in these circumstances, so he couldn't finish the season. Although he already had enough points to become world champion . . .'

'Go and get dressed,' Verity repeated more gently.

'Oh, Verity, you hardly know him . . .'

'I know him,' she said flatly. She knew him well enough to know he wouldn't do that, no matter what the provocation. Turning away, she filled the kettle and set it on the stove.

When Corbin came back, it was to an atmosphere that could have been cut with a knife. She and Stella had been shopping, eaten lunch, all in a semblance of normality, but both were feeling the strain. Stella kept trying to justify her belief in Corbin's guilt, Verity refused to discuss it. Corbin took one look at his mother's face, glanced at Verity, then said flatly, 'She told you.'

'Yes,' Verity said quietly.

'And?'

'And I don't believe a word of it,' she said with quiet conviction.

'Ah, yes, the famous intuition,' he said sarcastically. 'David told me about that.'

'Then maybe he also told you that I'm very rarely wrong. Have you eaten?'

'Yes.'

'Then if you'll excuse me, I still have to make the beds.' As she passed Stella, she halted. Touching a gentle hand to her shoulder, she smiled down at her. 'It's all right,' she said. 'Don't be upset.' Turning to Corbin, she added, 'Don't be angry with her; it was done from the best of intentions.'

Running swiftly upstairs, needing, wanting to be on her own, she went into her room and sat on the edge of the bed. Staring blankly at the window, she went over everything that Stella had said, about Eve, the crash, Corbin himself. She really had no idea why she was so convinced that the crash had been an accident. She had nothing concrete to base her feelings on, just a quiet conviction that she was right. And Eve? What was she like? As selfish and shallow as his mother had said? Being the wife of a racing driver wouldn't be easy but, whatever the difficulties, if you loved someone, you didn't have affairs with other men, and you most certainly didn't desert them when they needed you most.

And what had happened to her own policy of non-involvement? She clearly remembered her thoughts when she'd first met Corbin and it was decided she would work for him. He didn't need to like her, she'd told herself, any more than she needed to like him. Now her feelings weren't nearly so clear-cut. She'd been quite astonished by her anger that everyone should believe Corbin guilty. Astonished by the fierce protectiveness she'd felt. He was her employer, nothing more, nothing less. Well, maybe that wasn't quite true, she qualified honestly. She liked him, liked him very much. And that's as far as your thinking must go, Verity, old girl . . .

The sharp rap on the door startled her—and made her feel a touch of guilt. Hadn't done too much about making the beds, had she? With a little grimace she called, 'Come in.'

'Can I talk to you for a moment?' Corbin asked brusquely.

'Sure. Come in,' she said with a flippancy she was far from feeling. 'As you can see,' she murmured, indicating the untidy room, 'I haven't exactly been a busy bee since I left you.'

'No. Why didn't you believe my mother?' he asked abruptly as he came in and closed the door.

'Because I know you.'

'No, you don't! You know very little about me . . .'

'I know you wouldn't do that. No matter what the provocation,' she said quietly, her eyes not leaving his. 'So don't try to convince me otherwise, because I shan't believe you.'

Glaring at her, he walked moodily across to the window. Hands shoved into his back pockets, he stared out into the garden.

'You think I'm a fool, don't you?'

'No, why should I think you a fool?'

'Because of Eve, because I didn't fight to clear my name. Do you know why I didn't?' he asked, turning to face her.

'I can make a pretty good guess.' She smiled. 'One of my aunts, if she was in a temper, or cross, and you asked, "What's the matter?" would say grumpily, "If you don't know, I'm not going to tell you." '

Corbin gave a snort of laughter.

'I'm not altogether sure I like being lumped in with your aunt. But yes, something like that. At the initial hearing, I told them exactly what had happened—they looked so totally disbelieving, it was ludicrous. Innocent until proved guilty,' he murmured, 'Some joke . . .'

'So you lost your temper.'

'Yes,' he sighed. 'If they could automatically assume I was guilty, then to hell with them . . .'

'Including your mother?'

'Yes. No. Oh, hell, Verity, I don't know.'

'She's hurting very badly, Corbin,' she said gently. 'She loves you, wants you to be innocent, but is very afraid that you're not.'

'I know,' he agreed. 'Think I didn't know why she kept intruding into my life? Kept bringing an army of odd women?' Staring blindly across the room, he murmured almost to himself, 'Since the day she came to live with us . . .'

'Since the day . . .?' she echoed blankly.

'She's my stepmother,' he explained with a small smile.

'Your stepmother? But she never said . . .'

'No, she wouldn't. She likes people to think she's my mother—and you're not to tell anyone different. It's our little secret,' he said with another smile. 'I do love her, Verity—or at least, I'm extremely fond of her. My mother died when I was two, Dad married Stella when I was—oh, five or six, I think. She couldn't have any children of her own, and I became a sort of—I don't know, fixation, I suppose. She wanted to mother me, and the sad truth is, I hated it. I was never one for cuddles, being held in a strangled embrace. I like my own space around me, to make up my own mind slowly, cautiously, I suppose—and I used to get cross and shrug her away. Children can be unconsciously cruel. It wasn't because I didn't like her, I did, I just hated to be kissed and cuddled. Apparently she was very miserable for a while, until Dad explained to me why she was unhappy, and then I pretended. As well as I could, anyway.' And Verity had a mental image of the young Corbin screwing up his face and suffering his stepmother's hugs, then escaping as fast as he possibly could.

'And now she feels guilty that she not only failed you when you were small, but now . . .'

'Yes. She keeps trying to make things up to me, for things that were none of her doing . . .'

'Like Eve's defection?' she put in softly.

'You do stomp in where angels fear to tread, don't you?' he exclaimed, and when Verity gave an apologetic grimace he shrugged. 'Yes,' he admitted with a sigh, 'like Eve's defection. I knew what she was like, Verity,' he said quietly, his face distant, his eyes fixed on his feet. 'Shallow and selfish—only I wanted her—didn't want to be cautious. It was a recipe for disaster from the word go.'

'And you still love her,' she said flatly, then wondered why that should hurt her so much.

'Do I?' he said. 'I honestly don't know if it was ever love I felt for her. Want, need, overwhelming desire. I knew what she was like, yet I still wanted her. Now that, Verity, is a fool. Isn't it?'

'Is it? I don't know. How could I? I've never been in love. I don't know how it feels.'

'Wretched is how it feels. And stupid, and disgusted, and weak.' Shifting his stance, he returned his gaze to the window.

'And you hate yourself for it, don't you?'

'Yes, Verity, I hate myself—for the churning feeling in my insides whenever I even think of her. For the sleepless nights going over and over our marriage, trying to expunge my guilt . . .'

'Your guilt?' she exclaimed, astonished. 'From what I can gather, you have the least reason to feel guilty.'

'There were faults on both sides.'

'Possibly,' she murmured placatingly, privately thinking just the opposite. 'I'm sorry, Corbin. I wish I could help, but I'm a bit of a novice where affairs of the heart are concerned,' she said sadly, wishing for once in her life that she wasn't so inexperienced, that she could offer some concrete advice. Only she couldn't.

'Eve knows it, too,' he continued quietly. 'That I still want her. Oh, damn her, Verity. Damn her, damn her, damn her!' Then, with a crooked little smile, he remarked, 'Mother said she found herself telling you things without her ever meaning to—I now know what she meant. But that's as far as it goes, Verity. I never want to hear it discussed again! Not with anyone!'

'But you . . .'

'No,' he said flatly, and Verity gave him a disgusted look. 'The discussion is ended. Isn't it?'

'Yes,' she muttered reluctantly. 'But I still think . . .' only to abandon her argument when he glared at her.

'I promised Mother I'd take her for a drive,' continued Corbin blandly. 'Show her some of Britanny. Hardly the weather for it, but there you are. We'll have something to eat out.

Want to come?' he added as an obvious after-thought, and she shook her head.

'No. I have things to catch up on. Go on, you go. Have a good time.' His little laugh told her that he had no expectation of that at all.

She stayed where she was after he left—made no attempt to get on with her house-work. She had always been so sure of herself, of her ability to cope with whatever was thrown at her. Competent, self-contained, needing no one; yet now rather a lot of doubts were creeping in, as though all the things she had hitherto taken for granted were slowly being eroded. Poor Corbin. It must be terrible to love someone who didn't love back, or was incapable of loving back. It perhaps wouldn't have been so bad if Eve had been worth loving, but Verity didn't somehow think she was. She didn't ever remember feeling inadequate before, and it wasn't a feeling she enjoyed now. He deserved someone so much better than Eve. Someone warm and loving, patient with his moods, tolerant . . . Getting quickly to her feet, she stripped the bed with an angry movement, tossing the quilt and pillows across the room.

When she went down the next morning, it was to find Corbin and his mother already up. His mother's case was in the hall, her handbag lying on top. Pushing into the kitchen, she stared at them as they sat either side of the table.

'Are you leaving so soon?' she asked. 'We barely had a chance to get to know each other.' She was disappointed, she found. She'd liked her, enjoyed her company, despite their difference of opinion.

'Yes, dear, I'm going—to leave you both in peace. And, Verity—thank you,' murmured Stella awkwardly. 'Corbin and I had a long talk—and well, thank you.' And, taking Verity completely by surprise, she came across the kitchen and gave her a hug and a swift kiss on the cheek. 'We should have talked before— only people never do the obvious, do they? I would have gone on thinking he only suffered me because he thought he had to, and he would have continued to think I was a no-brain with the sensitivity of a brick.'

'I'm sure he didn't think any such thing,' Verity responded with a smile. 'Are you sure you have to go?'

'Yes, dear, I'm sure. But you will keep in touch?' she asked a little wistfully.

'Yes, I promise. Is Corbin running you to the airport?'

'Yes. Perhaps if you have some free time . . .' she began, then let her sentence trail off. With a deep breath and a determined smile, she looked at Corbin. 'Ready?'

'Sure.' With a vague smile at Verity, he escorted his mother out.

*   *   *

When he returned some hours later, he merely nodded to her, then disappeared into his study. Only it was clear he couldn't settle down to his book, because not half an hour later he wandered moodily into the kitchen.

'Have you eaten?' she asked quietly. If ever a man had something on his mind, that man was Corbin, and she eyed him curiously, wondering what was the matter.

Shaking his head, he leaned against the work surface. 'A snack will do, I'm not very hungry.'

'Omelette? Eggs on toast?'

'Mm, whatever.'

'Stuck?' she asked quietly.

'What?'

'The book, are you stuck?'

'Oh, no,' he mumbled, beginning to fiddle with the spatula she'd just taken out of the drawer.

Giving him a look of exasperation, she began whisking up the eggs with a great deal more energy than was needed. 'Your mother get off all right?' she persevered.

'Mm, yes, thanks. I promised to go and stay, next month, some time—soon . . .'

Dropping a blob of lard into the frying pan, Verity watched it sizzle and begin to smoke before pouring the eggs—and with the exact requirements of Sod's law the doorbell pealed.

'Oh, b . . .!'

'Verity!' he exclaimed.

'Well,' she said irritably, 'why couldn't they have rung before I put the eggs in?' Taking the pan off the heat, she walked quickly to the front door. A worthy young man stood there, notebook poised, and she didn't need a crystal ball to tell her who he was. A reporter. Now what?

'Yes?' she asked unhelpfully.

'McCaid about?' he asked flippantly.

'No, he isn't.' About to shut the door, she found his foot in the way, and added shortly, 'If you think those tactics will work with me, you're way off-beam. Move it!'

'OK, OK, keep your hair on. I only want to know where McCaid is.'

'I told you, out.'

'His car's outside . . .'

'So is the milk bottle—that doesn't mean I have the milkman here!'

'Oh, very funny—and just who the hell are you, anyway?'

'Goodbye,' she said flatly as she drew back the door to slam it on his foot.

'Wait!' he said hastily. 'Perhaps you can tell me his reaction to the news that Veroni has regained consciousness? Is he worried? Will there be an inquiry? Possible prison sentence . . .?'

'Mr McCaid was not responsible for the crash,' she said icily. 'And the only one who need worry about a prison sentence is you— for trespass!' With a movement too fast for him to anticipate, Verity kicked him hard beneath his kneecap, then slammed the door. Damned vultures! Turning quickly, she came face to face with Corbin. Raising her chin defiantly, she stared at him. He looked furious.

'Keep your nose out of my affairs, Verity. They're none of your business . . .'

'Neither are they any of his,' she muttered, indicating the recently departed reporter with a little toss of her head. 'And I don't know why you have to be so damned stubborn . . .'

'You don't know anything about it . . .'

'I know enough to know you should be out there denying it, instead of skulking in here!'

'I am not skulking!' he snapped.

Giving him a withering glance, she brushed past him and went into the kitchen.

'Verity,' he thundered, stalking after her, 'don't walk off when I'm talking to you!'

'Then don't talk rubbish!' she exclaimed fiercely. 'You had the perfect opportunity to deny you'd had anything whatever to do with Veroni's accident . . .'

'I am not talking to reporters!' he exclaimed furiously.

'Then don't! But when Veroni recovers he'll tell everyone it wasn't your fault, so I don't see . . .'

'Hah! If you think that, you have windmills in your head! Veroni hates my guts. Getting me a prison sentence, whether deserved or not, would give him untold pleasure!'

'Then all the more reason to stop hiding away like a criminal . . .'

'I am not hiding!' he shouted. 'I'm here to write a book!' Turning on his heel, he shoved his hands angrily into his back pockets and went to stare blindly from the window. 'And how the hell did he know where to find me?'

'Well, I don't know, do I? I didn't tell him!' Giving a long sigh, she stared at his rigid back. 'Look, Corbin,' she said more reasonably, 'you asked me to work for you . . .'

'Was asked to employ you,' he corrected coldly, and Verity pulled an exasperated face at his back.

'All right, whatever, but you also asked me to pretend an involvement with you, and that's a form of hiding. Behind me. Now, I know it was for pride's sake . . .'

'You don't know anything of the sort!' he gritted, turning a furious face to her.

'Yes, I do! Why can't you just tell them to go to hell and get on with your life?' she pleaded. 'You're not a coward, and it infuriates me when people think you are—and I'm damned if I'll stand by and watch them tear you to shreds without doing anything to help!'

'I don't want your help.'

'I don't care! You've got it, anyway?' Spinning round, she stormed out.

'Verity,' he roared, hastening after her, 'will

you just mind your own business?'

'No!' she shouted, swiftly climbing the stairs.

'Then you're fired! Do you hear me? Fired!'

'Good!' she yelled back, then squealed in alarm as her elbow was caught and she stumbled backwards. Cannoning into him, they both crashed into the wall at the bottom of the stairs.

CHAPTER SIX

OFF balance mentally as well as physically, Verity lifted wide, startled eyes to his face. Oh, lord, he looked as though he wanted to strangle her—then she jumped violently as the doorbell pealed.

'Corbin?' she whispered when he didn't react. 'The door . . .'

'Oh, go and answer the damned thing!' he muttered furiously. Shoving her almost violently away from him, he turned his back.

Taking a long, shuddery breath, she practically ran along the hall. If it was that damned reporter again . . .

'Hello,' a vision of loveliness murmured huskily, and Verity felt sorely tempted to slam the door in her face. She knew who it was. She'd never met her, never seen a photograph of her, but she knew instantly who it was. Eve. Corbin's ex-wife.

Green eyes flickered over her with an expression of amusement in their depths, before moving beyond her to Corbin, and Verity felt a violent desire to shove her backwards, off the top step. She had also apparently become invisible as she was thrust almost rudely aside and Eve advanced, arms outstretched towards Corbin in

what Verity privately considered to be a theatrical
display of very bad taste. However, she was
delighted to see that Corbin made no move
towards her, and not by the flicker of one eyelash
did he indicate any desire to see her.

'Eve,' he murmured flatly, neatly sidestepping
the perfumed embrace. Although Verity could no
longer see her face, she could picture the girlish
pout only too well. Pushing the door violently
shut with her foot, so that the echo reverberated
along the hall, she gave a saccharine smile as they
both looked at her.

'So sorry,' she apologised, 'my foot slipped.'

'Who is this person, Corbin?' Eve demanded
petulantly.

'This person,' Verity enunciated clearly,
'is——'

'Verity,' Corbin supplied hastily with a glare at
her. 'My—er—housekeeper.'

'Your housekeeper?' she exclaimed incredulously.

'A polite euphemism,' Verity murmured
sweetly as she walked past them. Widening her
eyes innocently at Corbin, she had the satisfac-
tion of hearing Eve choke.

'Corbin! You're never telling me she's your
mistress? *That* I won't believe! I mean, it's hardly
flattering to me . . .'

'He wasn't trying to flatter you, dear,' Verity
put in as she slipped into the kitchen, then smiled
ruefully as she heard Corbin snort with laughter.
Not that she was to be left in peace to enjoy her

triumph; both Corbin and Eve followed her in. Eve was very obviously trying to control her temper. And she'd be wise to do so, Verity thought, for losing her temper wouldn't earn her any brownie points.

'Don't I get offered a cup of tea or something?' Eve asked with an obvious attempt to get things back under control.

'We didn't think you'd be staying long . . .'

'Verity,' Corbin warned, 'be quiet.'

'Certainly. Would you like me to leave you alone?'

'It might make conversation easier, don't you think?' he asked smoothly.

As she closed the kitchen door behind her, she heard Corbin murmur blandly, 'She's incredibly jealous.'

Giving a little grunt of laughter, she walked slowly upstairs. Not that she was in the least amused; leaving those two alone together was a sure recipe for disaster. She hadn't missed the tension in him, even if Eve had, and his eyes, which lately had been warmer, softer, had looked bleak. Hunkering down on the top stair, she put her chin in her hands. So that was Eve. She might have the personality of a soup plate, but she was incredibly beautiful, there was no doubt about that. Did men really only care about looks? Conjuring up an image of her own ordinary face, she had to suppose they did. Certainly to date no one had declared an undying passion for *her*. She could hear the murmur of their voices, but not make out what they said, which was annoying. And why had she come? Surely not to ask him to take her back?

She didn't bother to move when she heard the kitchen door open, just watched morosely as they walked side by side up the hall, Corbin to open the front door, Eve to depart. As Corbin turned and saw her perched at the top of the stairs, he moved slowly to join her. He had a faint lipstick smear across his mouth.

'That shade of lipgloss doesn't suit you,' she said waspishly as he sat beside her.

'Jealous, Verity?'

'No. Why should I be jealous?'

'Mm. Why should you?' he asked softly, and she had a horrid suspicion he was laughing at her.

'You didn't tell me she was that beautiful,' she muttered.

'Remiss of me,' he drawled, and Verity could have hit him.

'Are you angry?' she probed. It was like talking to a damned brick wall. 'I was very rude.'

'Weren't you just?' As she peeped at him from the corner of her eyes, he added, 'And I'd very much like to know why.'

So would she. His ex-wife should have been a matter of complete indifference to her, but she wasn't. There was a hard, tight pain inside her and she didn't quite know how to disperse it. Fortunately, before she could provoke him further, the phone rang.

'Hell, aren't we to get any peace?' he muttered

wearily.

'I'll go.' Getting to her feet, feeling about a hundred years old, she walked down and picked up the phone.

'Bonjour . . .'

It was Corbin's mother, and as she listened to the excited babble at the other end she turned to stare at Corbin, a slow anger growing inside her. 'Yes, yes, I'll tell him, all right, bye.' She replaced the receiver. 'That was your mother,' she said flatly.

'So I gathered. What did she want?'

'For me to tell you that Veroni had apparently told the truth. You're in the clear. But then, you know that, don't you?'

'Yes,' he said baldly.

'That was why Eve came, wasn't it?' When he only continued to stare at her, his face devoid of expression, she burst out, 'Why didn't you tell me?'

'Why should I?'

Staring at him, suddenly feeling terribly hurt and bewildered, she echoed quietly, 'No. Why should you?'

Swinging round, she blindly grabbed her coat off the peg and pulled the front door open.

'Verity!'

Ignoring him, she slammed the door and took off down the street, her coat clutched to her chest.

She walked for a long time, aimlessly, without

direction, her mind blank. She'd totally lost her objectivity, she thought drearily, and that was a damn fool thing to do. That was the way to get hurt. Someone quiet, unobtrusive, he'd said. 'Then that's what I'll be,' she'd promised. Hah! Oh, really unobtrusive, Verity. Her feet automatically taking her back to the house some hours later, she suddenly remembered the omelette she'd been making and she gave a sad smile. A lot seemed to have happened since the making of the omelette.

Trailing miserably back to the house, she let herself quietly in. Corbin looked as though he'd been waiting for her.

'I'm sorry, Verity,' he said gently. 'I shouldn't take my bad temper out on you.'

'It doesn't matter,' she mumbled, making a great production of removing her coat.

'Of course it matters,' he said impatiently. 'It's quite obvious from your face that it matters.'

'No,' she said quietly, turning to face him. 'You have nothing to apologise for. You wanted someone quiet and unobtrusive, and all I've done so far is meddle in your affairs. I'm the one who should apologise. It won't happen again.' With a little nod, she slipped past him and went into the kitchen. His long sigh she ignored.

'Verity,' he began in exasperation as he followed her into the kitchen, 'I . . .'

'Leave it, Corbin, please. I don't want to talk

about it. Do you still want the omelette?'

'What? Oh, yes, if you like.' She was aware of him watching her as he sat at the kitchen table and began to play idly with the fork, but she kept her mind determinedly blank. She would be what she had promised. Quiet. Mouselike.

Unfortunately, Verity's decision not to become further involved wasn't as easy as she had thought it would be, and several times she'd had to bite her tongue to stop herself offering an opinion. It also became clear that Corbin too was finding the whole thing a severe strain on his nerves.

'OK,' he said, striding forcefully into the kitchen a few days later, 'I give in! I can't bear it any longer. Will you please send Verity back? This silent, unobtrusive, competent Miss Lang is driving me insane! I can't concentrate, I can't work, I sit staring at the wall, devoid of inspiration. I'm terrified to ask your opinion on anything . . .'

Staring at him, she suddenly gave a little grin, her eyes alight with laughter. 'All right,' she agreed softly. 'I have to admit I'm having an awful struggle myself.'

'Well, thank heavens for that!' he exclaimed. Beaming at her, he strode across and picked her up in a bear-hug. 'Let's eat out! I'm bored!'

Lauging, Verity agreed, and very foolishly didn't bother to analyse the reason for her happiness.

They managed two days of amity, which lately had to be some sort of record, before they were back at loggerheads. The reason was Pete Townley, the owner of the Cobra racing team, who arrived quite out of the blue. He was a very nice man, a little older than Corbin, fair hair brushed straight back, exposing his broad forehead and emphasising his bright, enquiring tawny eyes, Corbin greeted him rather warily.

'Hi,' he responded easily. Then, turning to Verity, he said, 'You'll be Verity. I saw Mrs McCaid, who extolled your virtues most thoroughly.'

Smiling every bit as warily as Corbin, Verity tried to excuse herself, only to be forestalled.

'It's nothing very private,' Pete Townley insisted easily. Then, turning to Corbin, he asked, 'So? When are you coming back?'

'I'm not. I told you.'

'Why?' he asked bluntly. 'Sulking, Corbin? I told you I'd resolve it, and I have.'

'What did you do? Threaten Veroni with dismissal from the team if he didn't agree to your terms?'

'Yes,' he agreed quietly. 'I told him I wouldn't have him back unless he exonerated you. Seeing as he wants to be next world champion and he has the best chance with my team, he agreed.'

'But Corbin was innocent?' Verity exclaimed, scandalised.

'I know—but without witnesses, it wasn't so easy to prove. I told old misery guts here to keep a low profile until I'd sorted everything out . . .'

Verity suddenly felt dreadful. That was why he didn't need her interference. It had all been in hand.

'. . . but I didn't intend for him to disappear from the face of the earth,' Pete continued drily.

'I didn't,' Corbin muttered moodily. 'I went to the States, stayed with Stella for a bit, then came here.'

'Didn't you trust me, Corbin?' Pete asked softly with a searching glance at the other man. 'I thought you understood. I had to keep it low-key, we didn't want a damned public inquiry, or the Press nosing around. I just miscalculated the time scale. I never thought Veroni would take so long to recover. Is that why you won't come back? To punish me?'

'No! You make me sound like a petulant child——' Breaking off, he gave Verity a swift glance, and his lips twitched.

Turning back to Pete, he gave him a rueful smile, 'Being away from it has given me time to think,' he continued. 'I'm thirty-four, a bit old to go careering round a track at goodness knows how many miles an hour.'

'But you love it, man!'

'I know,' he sighed, 'but even before the accident, I was seriously considering retiring. To be honest, I think I've lost the edge, the concentration . . .'

'Rubbish!' Pete exclaimed. 'You're the best damned driver there's been for years! Hell, Corbin, you can't give it up! Motor racing is your life! You don't know anything else.'

'Oh, I'll find something,' he replied with a warning glance at Verity.

Sighing, Pete ran his fingers through his hair, his face despondent. 'It's that bloody bitch, isn't it? I told you not to get involved with her . . .' Then, obviously realising that Corbin's clenched jaw hardly denoted agreement, he broke off, to mumble awkwardly, 'Well, don't dismiss it out of hand, think about it. Let me know in a week or so . . .'

'All right. But I won't make any promises.'

'Oh, well, I suppose I'll have to leave it at that. Your mother said you were coming to London next month?' When Corbin nodded, he added, 'Come and see me then, hm? We'll talk about it. Or is it that you're worried about Veroni?' he asked as an obvious afterthought.

'No, I'm not worried about Veroni,' Corbon said flatly, a rather hard light in his eyes.

No, but perhaps he was worried about Eve, Verity thought. Eve and Veroni had been very much involved with each other, if Stella McCaid was to be believed.

'OK. Ring for a cab for me, will you? I dismissed the one I came in. I expected a celebration,' grumbled Pete.

'Verity?' Corbin murmured.

'Sure.' With a small smile at the other man, she went out into the hall to ring for a taxi.

'It will be five minutes,' she told him on returning to the lounge, then wondered what they had been discussing so urgently and which necessitated breaking off in the middle when she returned. Eve?

Giving her a lame smile and a muttered 'thanks', Pete turned back to Corbin, 'I'll see you in London, then?'

'Mm.'

Then, with a rueful smile, Pete asked, 'Couldn't lend me the fare to get to the airport, could you? I don't have enough *francs.*'

'Sure.' Walking out to the hall, Corbin opened the drawer of the desk standing beneath the mirror. He frowned, pulled the drawer right out and scrabbled irritably in the muddle that accumulates in all drawers.

'Dammit, Verity,' he exclaimed, 'why didn't you tell me you'd used the money out of here?'

'Money?' she asked blankly. 'What money?'

'The money that I kept in this drawer for emergencies.'

'But I haven't used any money from there, Corbin,' she said quietly, her brows pulled into a frown.

'Then where is it?' he demanded, still scrabbling ridiculously in the drawer, as though it
would suddenly materialise.

'I don't know . . .'

'There aren't even any damned receipts,' he
muttered. As if that made any difference! she
thought in exasperation. Going back into the
lounge, she retrieved her handbag. Taking out
her purse, she handed Pete a wad of notes.

'That should be enough,' she murmured.

With a wry grimace at Corbin's back as he
still scrabbled through the drawer, Pete
whispered, 'I'm off. It was nice to meet you.
Maybe I'll see you in London.'

'Maybe,' she agreed.

'Bye, Corbin,' he mumbled hastily as he was
half-way out of the front door.

'What?' snapped Corbin, swinging round.
'Oh—bye. I thought he wanted some money?'
he demanded, as though the whole thing were
her fault.

'He did. I gave him some from my purse.'

'Well, I wish you'd remembered you'd put it
in there before I began scrabbling in this
damned drawer!' he said irritably, slamming it
shut.

'I didn't,' she said crossly. 'How many more
times do I have to tell you?'

'And I wish you'd leave receipts,' he carried
on, totally ignoring her denial. 'How the hell
am I supposed to account for money if you

don't leave receipts?'

'What receipts?' she asked in exasperation.

'The receipts for the money you used. Bills, accounts . . .'

'I know what receipts are, Corbin. I meant, why would I put receipts in the drawer when I didn't use that money?'

'You've been paying the bills, haven't you?'

'Yes, out of the money you give me each week.'

'Don't be ridiculous! That's your wages. I'm talking about the two thousand *francs* that were in the drawer!'

'Will you stop going on about that damned drawer? I just told you I didn't touch it!'

'Then where is it?'

'Well, I don't know, do I? Perhaps you used it and forgot . . .'

'I did not use it! Now, think! Who have you paid lately?'

'Corbin,' she retorted, her patience snapping, 'I've never been in that drawer, let alone touched the money. If I had, I'd have told you. Any bills I pay from the money you give me. Those receipts I keep in the kitchen.' Turning on her heel, she walked into the kitchen and across to the cupboard beside the sink, then retrieved the blue accounts book from the shelf. Marching back to him, she plonked it on the desk. 'Receipts,' she said shortly.

'Never mind the damned receipts! Just tell

me where the money went . . .'

'Corbin, I—did—not—use—it. Perhaps your mother borrowed it!'

'Why would my mother borrow it? If she needed money she'd ask me . . .'

'And I wouldn't?' she put in softly. 'Are you accusing me of stealing, Corbin?'

'No, I'm damned well not accusing you! I just want to know where it went. That's reasonable, isn't it?'

'Yes, it would be,' she said coldly, 'if I didn't keep getting the feeling you think I stole it for some nefarious purpose of my own.'

'Oh, to hell with it!' he snapped. Storming into his study, he slammed the door.

Only it wasn't the money, she knew that. It was Pete Townley's offer—and possibly his remarks about Veroni and Eve. If he went back to racing, with Veroni as his team-mate, that would bring them all back into contact again, and produce the same explosive situation there had been before. Sighing, Verity went into the kitchen and plumped down at the table. Perhaps he genuinely didn't want to go back to racing. As he'd said, thirty-four was old for a racing driver. And, as for the money, his mother had probably borrowed it the day they had gone shopping, and had forgotten to tell him. Certainly, she'd had some *francs* on her, and to Verity's knowledge she hadn't been to the bank to change any.

She stayed out of his way for the rest of the

day, finding reasons to be in parts of the house
where he wasn't likely to go. Perhaps they
needed a break from each other, she thought.
She'd been with him over a month without a
day off. Maybe that was it. Thinking about it,
she decided she'd ask for a couple of days off,
go and see Danielle. She hadn't seen her for
ages.

With sudden determination, she went along
to her room, threw a few belongings into a
holdall, then walked down to the study.
Tapping on the door, she walked in without
waiting for an invitation.

'I'm going away for a few days, Corbin. I
haven't had any time off since I've been here,
and I need a break,' she said bluntly. 'I'll be
back next Monday.'

Staring at her in astonishment, his brows
drawn into a frown, he demanded, 'Where are
you going?'

'To stay with Danielle for a few days.'

'Who the hell's Danielle?'

'An old friend. We met when I lived in
France when I was a child. We kept in touch.'

'Where does she live?'

'Carnac. Her parents own a *tabac* and bar
there.'

'And what am I supposed to do while you're
gone?' he demanded.

'Do about what?' she asked blankly.

'About everything! Food . . .'

'Oh, for pete's sake,' she exploded, 'you can

eat out, can't you?' Turning her back, she marched out, collected her bag and gave the front door a satisfying slam behind her. She felt ridiculously near to tears—and that infuriated her. She never cried.

Ringing her friend from a callbox in the town, she waited in a café for Danielle to come and pick her up. A few days of Danielle's no-nonsense company and she'd be as right as rain. Back to her usual self. Except she wasn't. She missed him. Ridiculous as it was, she missed him a lot. Even his temper. Not that Danielle seemed to notice anything amiss; she just chatted away in her usual fashion, pleased as always to see Verity—as were her parents. But the two days seemed to drag incredibly slowly. She was quite glad to return to Auray.

Corbin was waiting for her when she arrived back. Whether he'd seen her coming down the road, or whether he'd been waiting there for ages, she didn't know.

'Hello,' he murmured, looking thoroughly sheepish.

'Hello.'

'I found out who took the money,' he mumbled awkwardly. 'It was my mother. She borrowed it when you both went shopping. She rang the day after you left.' When she didn't comment, he sighed. 'I'm sorry, Verity.'

'It's all right——' she began, and he gave a snort of laughter.

'That sounds suspiciously like an Aunt Lucy sort of voice.' Spreading his hands helplessly, he added, 'I thought you might not come back.'

'Did you?' she asked unhelpfully, a wry smile in her eyes.

'Mm—but you have, haven't you?'

'Have I?'

'Verity! You don't want me to grovel, do you?'

'I might,' she announced, and he grinned, a wide, bright, happy grin, and she suddenly felt a hollow sort of pain inside. Looking down, she sighed. 'No, I don't want you to grovel, Corbin.' Handing him her holdall, she removed her coat.

'I missed you,' he said quietly. 'The place was like a damned morgue—it also got very untidy,' he confessed with a rather bewildered air, as though he couldn't possibly imagine how any such thing could have happened. 'I didn't realise how efficient you were until you'd gone! How in heaven's name did you hoover and keep the place clean without my hearing you?'

'I hoovered when you were out. If you didn't go out, I used a dustpan and brush,' she said evenly.

'Heavens! I didn't deserve you, did I?'

Giving a little smile, she replied quietly,

'Probably not.'

'But you will stay, won't you?'

'I suppose so,' she agreed, knowing it was really what she wanted. She didn't think she'd realised quite how much she had missed him until she saw him again. Yet how foolish, she thought, to become fond of him, and return to a house that was beginning to feel like home. When he'd finished his book, they would leave, go their separate ways.

'Why don't you go into the lounge?' he persuaded. 'I'll make you a cup of tea.'

Giving a little snort of laughter, Verity went obediently into the lounge and sat down. With a little twitch of her lips, she stared round her at the tidy room. He had been busy. When he came in with the tea-tray, she was laughing softly.

'What?' he asked.

'Just amused by your spurt of domesticity,' she murmured teasingly.

Giving her a wry grin, he relaxed back into the comfortable armchair. 'I've been up since five,' he admitted with a smile. 'Had a massive clear up. Hoovered, washed up. I even,' he grinned, 'put clean sheets on the beds.'

'And did the washing?' she teased.

'No,' he laughed, 'I couldn't figure out how to work the washing machine.'

Tilting her head on one side, she asked softly, 'Why the solicitude, Corbin? It just isn't like you.'

'I thought you'd take one look at the mess I'd made, and promptly leave again,' he confessed. 'It was pretty much of a tip. I also thought we might have lunch together.'

'Why?' she asked quietly.

'Because I feel guilty,' he murmured. 'Not a feeling I enjoy very much——' Then, his eyes filled with teasing humour, he added, 'I thought it would be a nice gesture.'

'And I would be overwhelmed and thank you nicely, and everything would go on as it did before?'

'Mm.' As though embarrassed, he got quickly to his feet. Taking a cheque from the mantelshelf, he handed it to her before sitting down again. It was for nine hundred *francs*.

'What's this for?' she asked, puzzled.

'The money you spent out of your wages on shopping, bills.'

'But I don't want it. You pay me far too generously, Corbin . . .'

'I pay you what you're worth,' he said firmly. 'Now, if you've finished your tea, go and get ready and I'll take you out to lunch.'

'Yes, Corbin,' she said obediently.

CHAPTER SEVEN

NOW that she was back, Corbin seemed oddly contented—relaxed, even amiable; or maybe that was conceit on her part, maybe it was just that the book was going well. He seemed to be getting on with his typing all right, she could often hear him tap-tapping away. He also seemed to accept that he was newsworthy, that there was bound to be speculation about whether he would go back to motor racing. Sometimes a reporter would ring, and on occasion Corbin would even take the call; yet Verity found herself watching him, waiting almost, and she had no idea why she felt so unsettled. She felt protective towards him, and that should have amused her, only it didn't. The weather, too, had changed. As January limped into February, the rain returned. The wind was colder, the clouds darker, heavier, and it seemed that at the least provocation they would empty their burden to fill gutters and streams, and swell the river. The steep little cobbled street became a nightmare to negotiate, and Verity was forced to invest in a pair of ridge-soled boots. She also bought herself a hat. It wasn't exactly a Paris creation, and looked rather as though it might have been rejected by just about everybody. It was crumpled and sad-looking, and she fell in love with it. It was a bright red cloche sort of hat, and it drooped round her ordinary face and made people laugh. It also made her feel happy, which was good; she hadn't seemed to feel very happy for a long time.

'Good lord, Verity!' Corbin exclaimed the first time he saw her wearing it. 'Whatever have you got on your head?'

'Don't you like it?' she asked, peering into the hall mirror, her head on one side.

'No. It makes you look like a bewildered mushroom.'

Turning, she tugged it more firmly over her ears, her eyes alight with laughter. 'It keeps me warm,' she retorted. Then, with a wide, delightful grin, she added, 'It cheers people up no end; even the gloomiest face breaks into a smile when they see me. So you see, it's a very useful sort of hat.'

'But it doesn't suit you . . .'

'No hats suit me, so I plumped for one that was dashing instead. I love it!' she exclaimed happily.

Shaking his head at her, he carefully removed it. 'Well, I don't think you need to wear it indoors. Now, are you busy?'

'No. I don't need to put the dinner on yet. Why? Did you want something?'

'Mm, a favour.'

'OK.' Taking her hat from him, she folded it carefully and put it on the hall table, then gave it a fond little pat. 'What do you want me to do?'

'I've finished the first draft of the book,' he mumbled, giving her a wry look. 'Will you read it? Give me your opinion?'

'Me?' she exclaimed, astounded. 'Oh, Corbin, that's a hell of a responsibility. I'm no expert on what's good or marketable.'

'I'd still like you to read it.'

'But surely a publisher would be the best person . . .'

'No! Hell, Verity, if it's rubbish, then at least I won't have gone to the embarrassment of submitting it.'

'But you don't have to send it in under your own name.'

'Yes, I do. It was commissioned,' he admitted, glaring at her. Waiting for her to laugh? she wondered.

'Do you think it's good?' she prevaricated.

'I don't know,' he confessed, giving a despondent sigh. 'I thought so at first, but the more I read it, the worse it gets. Please? I really would value your opinion.'

'All right,' she agreed reluctantly, not sure she was being altogether wise. Suppose it was dreadful? How would she be able to tell him?

'I'll go and get it.'

'What, now?'

'Yes.'

'Oh, hell. Crossing her fingers, Verity followed him into the study where, with a rather fatalistic gesture, he handed her a bulky stack of paper.

'I'll go out. Er—I'll—um—see you later,' he mumbled awkwardly.

'All right,' she said quietly.

When he'd gone, she sat in the leather armchair beside the fireplace and held the manuscript on her knee for a good five minutes before daring to look down at it. Then, taking a deep breath and sending up a little heartfelt prayer that it would be good and she wouldn't have to lie to him, she started on the first page.

She didn't hear him return, didn't hear the study door open. Her body tense, she read the last page quickly, frantically almost, quite unaware that her face was wet with tears.

'Verity!' he exclaimed. 'What in heaven's name's the matter?'

Startled, she looked up, her eyes blank.

'Verity?' he said more gently, coming to kneel in front of her. 'Is it so very terrible?'

Shaking her head, she swallowed hard before wiping her fingers across her damp cheeks in a surprised little gesture. 'It made me cry,' she murmured huskily.

'But why?'

'I thought he was going to die.' Then, with a lame smile, she leaned back with a long sigh. 'Oh, Corbin.'

'Is that a good "Oh, Corbin" or a bad "Oh, Corbin"?' he asked tentatively.

'Don't you know?' she asked softly, and when he shook his head she reached out to lay a gentle hand on his cheek. 'It's beautiful. Brilliant—oh, Corbin,' she said helplessly, 'I was so terrified I wouldn't like it, terrified of having to lie to you, and now I can't find the words to tell you . . .'

'Does that mean it's all right?' he asked hopefully.

'Oh, yes,' she said fervently. 'Very much all right.' Searching his eyes which today looked as blue as a summer sky, she suddenly felt absurdly shy, overwhelmed almost at being in the presence of someone who could write so powerfully. 'You mustn't change anything. Send it just as it is.'

'Really all right?' he persisted.

'Really—I wouldn't say so otherwise.'

His face serious, he framed her face with his large palms, his eyes holding hers. 'Thank you, Verity. I have to confess I was absolutely terrified. I've been walking round the town, staring at things without seeing them, trying to picture your reactions.' With a funny little sigh, he gave her a shaky grin. 'Thank you.' Leaning forward, he touched his mouth to hers in a warm, gentle kiss that made her heart race. Then he asked teasingly, 'Did you like the bit about the girl learning to drive?' And she gave a soft laugh.

'Yes.' Sobering, she asked, 'Corbin, why did you call her Lange? Coincidence?'

'What do you think?'

'I don't know,' she whispered.

'Don't you? I was going to call her Verity, but I thought you might object.'

'Why?'

'Why did I think you might object?' he asked humorously.

'No, silly, why would you have called her Verity?'

'As a sort of thank you. I couldn't have done it without you, you know.'

'Of course you could! I didn't do anything.'

'Yes, you did. You gave me peace and quiet, confidence . . .'

'Confidence?' she asked, astonished. 'How did I give you confidence?'

'I don't know, really,' he said slowly. 'But before we came here, before I met you, I'd been trying to write, getting angry with myself, thinking it was hopeless, yet once we were here, everything seemed to fall into place. So thank you, Verity. I even made her look like you,' he murmured with a smile. 'Didn't you notice?'

'No!' she exclaimed, embarrassed. 'The girl in your book was beautiful . . . so don't try your flattery on me, Corbin McCaid!' she said almost fiercely. 'By no stretch of the imagination could I be called beautiful.'

'Says who? Admittedly, the first time I met

you I didn't think so, but now . . .' He broke
off, his head on one side. 'Now—well, now
you're just my Verity,' he teased. 'And you are
lovely. Especially as you like my book.'
Grinning, he got to his feet and, taking the
manuscript from her lap, he put it on the desk.

Staring at him, at the foolish smile playing
about his mouth, she suddenly realised
something she should have realised a long time
ago.

'I'll go and start the dinner,' she said
abruptly. Getting swiftly to her feet, she
hastened into the kitchen, and then just stood,
staring at nothing. She felt as though she were
shaking inside, her mind unfocused. You're in
love with him, she told herself faintly. When
he kissed you, you wanted to fling your arms
round his neck, hold him tight, kiss him back.
No! Oh, dear heaven, no. Walking shakily
across to the table, she sank weakly down on
one of the chairs. Her hands clenched in her
lap, she stared out through the window, and
didn't even see the low, angry clouds that
raced across the sky, the trees dripping
moisture on to the wet lawn. It's because of
the book, she tried to tell herself. The warmth
and the passion in it, the excitement, the
danger, the sadness, that's all it is. Only it
wasn't. She knew it wasn't. Why had she never
realised that the pleasure she felt in his
company was because she was falling in love
with him? Why didn't she realise that was the

reason she had missed him when she'd gone away? Because she hadn't wanted to admit it, she told herself honestly. And the love passages in the book, that was why they had hurt, because she thought they might have been based on Corbin's experiences with his wife. He might have made the heroine look vaguely like herself, but wasn't she really based on Eve? They'd been very descriptive, those passages. Not crudely so, but beautifully written, compassionate, exciting. Clenching her hands tighter until the nails dug into her palms, she screwed her eyes tight shut for a moment, to shut out her visions of Corbin and his beautiful wife entwined on a wide bed. His mouth on hers.

She couldn't stay, not now, not with the knowledge that she loved him eating away her insides. How could she face him for days? Weeks? Or did she even need to? Now that his book was finished, he wouldn't need her any more, would he?

Getting stiffly to her feet, she walked across to the vegetable rack. 'Dinner,' she told herself firmly. 'Just get the damned dinner.'

The next few days took on the semblance of a nightmare as she tried never to be alone with him. He gave her some odd looks sometimes as she dashed out of a room he'd just come into, or she was more abrupt than usual, but he was immersed in doing the finishing touches to his book and presumably dismissed her odd behaviour from his mind. And perhaps she only thought he looked at her oddly because she was conscious of how she'd changed. He probably didn't notice anything at all. She prayed that was so anyway; she couldn't have borne an inquisition on her behaviour. Even the red hat couldn't drag her out of her depression. Yet something good happened, too. An ordinary outing to the shops brought her unexpected pleasure.

As she was fighting her way up the hill from the quay, she paused as she often did, to peer into the window of the gallery, and there, tucked away at the back of the cluttered window, was a picture she recognised. For a moment she thought she was imagining it; then, with heart racing, she went inside. Staring at it almost in disbelief, a silly smile on her face, she bought it. Holding it carefully beneath her raincoat to keep it dry, she hurried up the hill to the house. Almost sneaking up to her room, she pulled off her coat and balanced the picture carefully on the dressing-table. Staring at it, her eyes filled with silly tears.

'Hello. I didn't hear you come in!' Corbin exclaimed from the open doorway, and before Verity could react he'd walked in to stand behind her kneeling figure. 'Good lord, Verity! Have you just bought that? It's awful.'

'Yes,' she murmured huskily.

'But what on earth possessed you?' he asked in astonishment, perching on the end of the bed to get a better view. 'I don't even know what it is!'

'A yacht,' she said quietly.

'Oh, surely not.' He grinned, putting a warm hand on her shoulder. 'Are you sure it's not upside-down?'

'No.'

'Well, I don't think it's a yacht, Verity,' he murmured, peering almost cross-eyed at the blobs of yellow and green and brown. 'I think it's meant to represent mud.'

'No,' she denied again softly, her wide eyes fixed on the picture, 'it represents pleasure, and laughter—fish soup and crusty bread. It represents silly jokes and teasing . . .' It was so clear in her mind, that evening that her father had erupted into the house. His astonishment and pleasure that someone had bought his painting, had actually wanted it. Of her mother laughing uproariously, telling him there must have been a mistake. Of her ten-year-old self hunched up on the sofa, watching them, their closeness to each other. Had that unknown purchaser known it was of a yacht? she wondered. And how had it come to be in a little unknown gallery in Auray?

'Verity?' Corbin queried softly, hunkering down beside her and turning her face towards him. 'Tears, Verity?' he asked, wiping a gentle thumb across her tear-stained cheek. 'That's

twice I've found you crying.' Turning his gaze
back to the painting, he bent to read the
scrawled signature at the bottom. 'J Lang,' he
murmured. 'He was your father?' he asked,
turning to search her misty eyes.

'Yes.'

'I'm sorry. It's a lovely painting.'

'No, it isn't,' she said, giving him a watery
smile. 'It's a terrible painting—but it's
beautiful too, because he put love into it. It
might not look like the yacht it was meant to
represent, but it was painted with such pride,
such care—and it's all I have of him.' Giving a
funny little sniff, she turned away from his
penetrating gaze to search for a hanky.
Blowing her nose hard, she sat back on her
heels to stare once more at the swirling browns
and yellows.

'Tell me about him, Verity,' Corbin urged
softly.

Staring at the painting, her mind winging
backwards, she gave a faint reminiscent smile.
'He was tall, big, larger than life; the
unlikeliest candidate for bank manager that
you would ever meet. Yet he loved it. He also
loved to paint. He didn't have an artistic bone
in his body, but he adored it. Perhaps it was
living in France which brought out a latent
artistic streak, I don't know. I don't remember
that he used to dabble before we moved to
Paris so that Dad could manage that branch of
his bank when I was six. Whatever, every spare

moment he had, he'd go out with his easel. My mother used to tease him unmercifully—but in a fond, loving way—not that he cared. I went to a little school for English children run by nuns; surprisingly, there were quite a few of us. I loved it, loved Paris, the Brittany coast for holidays. Then, when I was eleven, they died. In a car crash. I was at school, I was doing a maths test, I remember, when I was sent for.' Giving a small sad sigh, she continued, 'I was sent back to England to my father's sister. Very opinionated was Aunt Lucy,' she recalled with a little laugh. 'She had two large sons and a daughter a few years older than me. They were all exceptionally clever. Very fond of handing out advice to their little dumb cousin.'

'And the dumb little cousin nodded, smiled, agreed, and went her own sweet way?' he asked with a smile.

'Mm. Did exactly what she wanted to do, when she wanted to do it—quietly.' She gave a little grin to show she was only half joking. 'Anyway, their advice was based on how they would react to a given situation, not how I would react—so it didn't really apply, did it? And I'm perfectly amiable, you know—as long as my interests don't clash with anyone else's.'

'And you look so gentle, too,' he teased. 'Such a little mouse.'

'Well, mice are pretty quiet,' she agreed.

'They also do pretty much as they like . . .'

'Until a large cat comes along,' he said drily.

'Until a large cat comes along,' she echoed.

'And that's why you said to me that first time we met that you would be whatever I wanted you to be. Because there wasn't anyone else you wanted to be at that particular time.'

'Mm hm.' She grinned.

'Until the first night, when the image slipped just a trifle?' he went on, tongue very firmly in cheek.

Laughing, she punched him playfully on the arm.

'But didn't living with them make you more determined to have a place of your own one day? So that you could do as you pleased, not what pleased everyone else?' he asked curiously.

'No, oddly enough, it didn't. I think I got so used to travelling light. I never had many things of my own—books, toys—that I needed a home for. I don't seem to accumulate things like other people, and mostly any presents I got were clothes, money . . .'

'But what happened to all the things you had before your parents died?'

'Oh, Aunt Lucy decided they should be thrown away. It would be too upsetting, she said, to keep them—maudlin . . .

'What a cow,' he said explicitly, and Verity smiled at him.

'Yes, I must admit I've never forgiven her for that.'

'Do you still see them?'

'My cousins sometimes. They did their duty by me.'

'And never let you forget it, by the sound of it.'

'No. I struck out on my own as soon as I left school, and although I'd learned shorthand and typing, I became a chambermaid in a hotel.'

'So that you could live in and solve the problem of accommodation?'

'Yes. I did a course in hotel management, went round various hotels, then two years ago I met David. He was interviewing in one of the hotels—I applied for the job—and here I am.'

'And here you are,' he echoed.

A sudden gust of wind rattling the window brought her out of her reverie, and she became aware of how close Corbin was to her. One blunt-fingered hand was resting on the edge of the dressing-table, near enough for her to reach out and touch. With an abrupt movement, she got to her feet. 'Did you send off your manuscript?' she asked with a hasty change of subject.

'Mm? Oh, yes. All registered.' He smiled. 'Now we only have to wait.'

'Not long, I suspect. They'll snap it up.'

'So sure, Verity?'

'Mm. So sure. Now, I went out to get

something for dinner—and came home with a painting instead.' She forced herself to sound light-hearted. Grabbing her mac from the bed, suddenly feeling stifled at being forced to be in the same small room as Corbin, especially the bedroom, she quickly walked across to the door and opened it. 'I won't be long.'

'Verity?' he called, forcing her to halt. 'Have I done something to upset you? I get the distinct feeling you're avoiding me.'

'Avoiding you? Why should I be avoiding you?' she asked stiffly, keeping her eyes firmly averted from his face.

'That's what I'd like to know. It's seemed lately that every time I come into a room, you quickly go out. Today's the first time in a week that you've actually stayed put long enough for us to have a conversation.'

'Don't be silly. It's your imagination. I won't be long.' Hastily escaping, she ran down the stairs and out of the front door. The sudden strength of the wind gave her thoughts a new direction, and she didn't have time to consider their conversation as she battled her way up the cobbled hill to the town. But it was there, in the back of her mind, just waiting for the opportunity to pop out, which came as she was wandering rather aimlessly round the *supermarché*. Now that he'd finished his book, she should tell him she was leaving. And then, get out of his life before she got badly hurt. Resolutions were all very well, she thought with a sigh, so long as you could put them into practice.

She lingered as long as she dared over choosing meat and vegetables for their dinner, and it was almost dark when she turned for home, most of the shops already shut for the afternoon. Even then, she didn't go straight back, but lingered in the café over a cup of coffee. She really should leave, she thought despondently, should tell him when she went back. The trouble was, she didn't want to, but how much longer could she go on pretending that all was well? She wasn't a very good actress, and it was becoming desperately hard not to let him see how she felt about him. It would be too mortifying if he found out, especially as she had the horrid suspicion he would go back to Eve.

With a long sigh, she tugged her hat more firmly round her ears and went out to do battle with the elements again. The wind had got stronger, if anything, and the few people still out were staggering about as though drunk. With her shopping clasped to her chest with one hand, the other holding her hat on, she made her way towards the quay. It was as she was staggering down the cobbled hill, against the wind, towards the house, that she gradually became aware of something not quite normal. She could hear faint shouts borne on the wind, saw a sudden flare of light as though someone had switched on a heavy beam, which just as suddenly went out. As she reached the house, Georges Martin, from the house across the way, suddenly erupted out of his front door and began to run awkwardly down towards the river. Puzzled, Verity dumped her shopping behind the wall in her front garden and followed him.

As she reached the end of the lane, the wind suddenly changed direction and nearly swept her off balance. Grabbing the shutter on the front of the art shop, she peered across to the river. Her first thought was, what damned idiot was trying to steer a yacht upriver in this weather? Her second, immediately on the heels of the first, had her gasping with shock as she realised it was totally out of control. The wind seemed to have shifted it beam-on, and as if in slow motion it began to topple, and she saw to her horror that the floating restaurant had broken its mooring and had swung out to hole the yacht. There were figures on both sides of the river, shouting instructions, which even to her untutored ear sounded contradictory, and then she saw what everyone else was pointing at. As the yacht slowly heeled over, she saw three life-jacketed figures clinging precariously to the rail before they were catapulted into the racing river.

Letting go of the shutter, she lurched and staggered across the road and on to the path, then felt her heart dip alarmingly as she recognised Corbin. He'd already shrugged out of his coat and shoes, and cold terror clutched at her. No, she thought. Oh, no. But it was too late, he was already diving and she frantically switched her attention to the river. Two orange life-jackets were within his reach, a third was already spinning towards the bridge. Hardly even aware of what she was doing, she began running, removing her coat, dragging off her boots. She vaguely heard someone yell, 'No-o!' and then the cold, angry water was closing over her head. And it *was* cold, heart-numbingly cold; for a second she couldn't think, couldn't breathe, as the icy water seemed to squeeze the life from her lungs. If the orange life-jacket hadn't bumped against her, she'd probably have done nothing, she thought afterwards. With an instinct borne of desperation, she grabbed at it, caught hold, and was swept helplessly towards the bridge. She had enough gumption left to know that if she hit the arch she would be killed, and with numbing slowness she managed to twist herself round so that, if she hit it, it would be feet first. And then it was too late to think of anything, as they were hurled into the maelstrom of white water as it rushed beneath the narrow bridge. To the left, her mind screamed, keep to the left, there was a pile of rocks, if she could . . .

Her outstretched legs hit it with a bone-jarring crunch, and then hands were grabbing her, taking her burden, hauling her out, holding her. Shivering uncontrollably, coughing up foul-tasting water, she was vaguely aware of a blanket being wrapped round her before strong arms swept her up.

'Bloody fool, damned stupid little fool.' Over and over, those meaningless words, which were spoken in Corbin's voice. Once the knowledge penetrated that he was all right, she gave herself up to her shivers, her teeth clacking like castanets, her throat and chest aching from her retching.

He took her up to the house, upstairs, into his bathroom. Verity was vaguely aware of what was happening, only her mind wouldn't latch on to it. Water running, rough hands stripping her, dumping her in hot water.

'Can't . . .' she began weakly.

'Shut up,' he said tersely.

Then the water was up to her chest, neck, and she gasped with shock as Corbin climbed in beside her, held her, pushed her head beneath the water before dragging her upright again and holding her tight.

'I'm all right,' she spluttered.

'You're not all right,' he denied angrily. 'You're half bloody drowned, frozen to death, cut, bruised . . .'

'Cut?' She frowned. She wasn't cut, just wet, then retched weakly as a foul taste filled her throat. As though she were a mere slab of meat, she was hauled roughly out and wrapped in a dry, warm towel; another was wrapped round her soaking hair, and he carried her into his room, put her into his bed.

'Verity, I could kill you!'

'You did it,' she muttered.

'Is that any reason for you to be so stupid? If I put my hand in the fire, would you do like-wise? Get under the covers,' he muttered brusquely. 'And don't move. I'll make us a hot drink!'

Ungluing her eyes, she stared at him. He was naked, roughly towelling himself with a blue towel, hard, rough strokes—to get his circu-lation going, she supposed vaguely. Then he was shrugging into his dressing-gown, black, not silk . . .

'Wake up,' he said abruptly, his voice intrusive, harsh. 'Come on, Verity, you have to drink this.'

Mumbling tiredly, her body still cold and shivery, she felt him lift her and she reluctantly opened her eyes. 'Come on, there's a good girl,' he persuaded, holding a cup to her lips. Struggling to free her arms from the quilt, she grasped the cup and drank.

'Come on, all of it,' he insisted, holding her upright with one arm, the other tilting the mug.

'Can't.'

'Can,' he contradicted.

'Bully.'

'Shut up and drink.'

As soon as she'd finished, he stacked pillows

behind her, unwound the towel from her hair
and began rubbing it briskly.

'Ouch, you're hurting . . .'

'Serves you right,' he muttered unfeelingly,
'but you can't go to sleep with wet hair.'

'It's not bedtime.'

'It is for you. Now, keep still. Do you have a
hairdryer?'

'In my room.' The minute he released her,
she curled back under the covers and began to
drift into sleep. She was only hazily aware of
him returning, of the hum of the hairdryer,
warm air on her scalp, and then nothing.

Drifting up out of sleep, she became aware of
a warm body close to her, of her own naked-
ness, of a small lamp burning on the bedside
table. Snuggling against the warmth, only half
awake, she traced her hand over a smooth,
warm chest, felt warm breath drift over her
face. Slowly she opened her eyes.

'How do you feel?' Corbin asked softly.

'OK,' she whispered. He was leaning up on
one elbow, looking down at her, his eyes bluer,
warm, soft. With a funny little smile, she
closed her eyes again—then snapped them
open in shock.

'The river!' she gasped, as everything that
had happened came rushing back. 'The
people . . .'

'All safe. Oh, Verity, when I heard them
shout, saw the damned red hat go into the

river—I thought . . .' And his voice cracked
for a moment. Sighing, he traced a gentle
finger across her face.

'I didn't think,' she murmured, 'I saw you
go in . . .'

'I was on a rope, dammit!'

'Oh.'

'Yes, *oh*. If you hadn't hit that rock by the
outlet pipe, if they hadn't dragged me to the
bank so quickly . . . Hell, Verity, I've never
run so fast in my life. We dashed along that
bank like Olympic athletes, even old Georges.
We jumped down on to the rock and just
grabbed you both—how the hell we didn't all
overbalance back into the river, I'll never
know!' Taking a long, ragged breath, he
gently touched her face again. 'Yet, if you
hadn't been so impulsive, that little girl would
have died. The river was too swift, too high,
we'd never have reached her.' With a little
smile, he hugged her to him and rubbed his
face against hers.

'It was so cold,' she murmured stupidly, her
body reacting quite independently to his naked
warmth as she slid her palms across his
shoulders. 'I never thought it would be so
cold. I couldn't swim or anything, it just
numbed me. I can't believe I did anything so
stupid. I didn't even know it was a little girl.
She is all right?'

'Mm, in the hospital with her parents—
they'll be fine,' he mumbled, his voice as

absent as her own. As he shifted his body, she felt the hard warmth of him against her and she wasn't so innocent that she didn't understand what was happening to him.

'I want you,' he admitted ruefully as he saw the bright knowledge of awareness in her eyes. 'Want to make love to you—only that's not fair, is it? You've been saving yourself . . .'

'Not saving,' she denied huskily. 'Never met anyone I wanted in that way.' She didn't want to talk, just wanted to hold him, have him kiss her, and she lifted her head slightly to touch her mouth to his. 'Oh, Corbin,' she sighed. His mouth was warm, dry, his body hard, exciting, yet the moment she tried to burrow closer to his warmth he shifted away.

'I should have worn my dressing-gown,' he whispered. 'Only I didn't want to. I wanted to feel you against me, your soft, warm skin.' And Verity thought she might faint from the feelings rioting inside her. She didn't think she could speak, her throat felt too dry, and her eyes felt too big for her face as she gazed up at him.

'I've been lying here, watching you sleep, thinking over all that happened, wanting to keep you safe.' He gave a self-deprecating smile. 'Think I'm daft, don't you?' And she shook her head weakly. 'My Verity,' he murmured softly. Bending his head, he touched his mouth softly to each eyelid, then moved to her mouth, and Verity drew her arms out from under the covers and wound them round his neck in silent invitation. If he didn't love her, so what? She wanted him. There was a fierce ache inside her for this man, and she had a horrible feeling that no one else would ever make her feel like this. It was just her misfortune to love where it wasn't returned. But he was fond of her, she thought, and he'd be a gentle and considerate lover. There were a great many women who never experienced that.

'You're not on the Pill, are you, Verity?' he asked softly.

'No,' she murmured, her eyes fixed on his face, a sinking feeling beginning inside her.

'No.' Sighing, he gently pushed her tangled hair from her face, his expression gentle, kind. 'It wouldn't be fair, Verity, and much as I long to be selfish . . .' With a small smile, he added, 'Maybe I'm not such a bastard, after all.'

'I never thought you were,' she mumbled unhappily. Should she beg him? Tell him it was what she wanted more than anything else in the word? 'Corbin?'

'Hush,' he said gently. 'Don't tempt me. I think if I did what I wanted, what you think at this moment you want, I'd end up hating myself. Keep it for a man you can love—who will love you.'

'But I do love you!' she exclaimed without thinking. Then, seeing the pain in his eyes, she whispered, 'Oh, damn you, Corbin.' With a little cry, she scrambled from the bed and dashed into the bathroom. Slamming the door behind her, she collapsed in a crumpled heap on the floor and began to cry: racking, tearing sobs that tore through her slight frame. And she couldn't stop. Much as she wanted to, she couldn't stop. Grabbing the edge of the bath, her fingers painfully tight on the porcelain, she rested her head on her arms and cried.

'Oh, darling, don't,' he said thickly, bending to cradle her in his arms. 'Don't.'

'No,' she gulped. 'It's the shock, I expect.' And her voice was quavery, uncertain, distorted by tears.

'Yes.' She was grateful that he pretended to believe the small lie. 'Come on,' he murmured, lifting her and carrying her back to the bed. 'You'll catch cold.' Tucking her back beneath the quilt, he laid a gentle hand against her cheek before shrugging into his dressing-gown. 'It's best, Verity,' he said softly, perching on the edge of the bed, his face haunted.

Staring at him, her eyes red and puffy, she whispered, 'You're still in love with her, aren't you? Hoping to get back together.' And she knew it was the truth by the way he avoided looking at her.

'I'm sorry, Verity,' he said miserably. 'I wouldn't hurt you for the world—and I shouldn't have had you in my bed. But, oh, Verity, I'm only human, and it's been such a long time . . .'

'I know. Don't say any more. Please.'

'Men are so bloody selfish!' he said bitterly.

'It's all right, Corbin, truly,' she soothed, laying a gentle hand on his arm.

'And I don't deserve that, do I? Not from you.' Taking a ragged breath, he got to his feet.

CHAPTER EIGHT

'WANT to stay in bed? Or get dressed?' asked Corbin quietly.

'I'll get up,' Verity murmured.

'OK. I'll go and make some coffee.'

When he'd gone, she got slowly out of bed. She was cut, she saw; there was a long gouge on her thigh, cuts and bruises by her ankle. Giving them no more than a cursory glance, she trailed out and across to her room. Collecting clean underwear, jeans and a sweater, she went along to the bathroom to shower and wash her hair. Don't think, she admonished herself. Blank it out.

When she went down, Corbin told her to go into the lounge. 'I've lit the fire. Go and get warm, Verity; I'll bring the coffee through. Want something to eat?'

Shaking her head, she went into the lounge and sat in the armchair that had been pulled up to the fire. Gazing blankly into the dancing flames, she thought about the incident in the river, the people, anything to keep her mind off Corbin and Eve.

'They are all right?' she asked listlessly as Corbin carried in the tray.

'Yes. I rang the hospital earlier. They're fine. Stay put,' he said as the doorbell rang. 'I'll go.' Putting the tray on the coffee table, he went out to answer the door. She heard mumbled voices, but she wasn't really interested.

'It was Georges,' he told her quietly. 'He brought in the shopping you left in the front garden—and this,' he added softly.

Looking up, she gave a small smile. Holding out her hand, she took the red hat from him. 'Where did he find it?'

'Some children found it upriver, they thought it might belong to the people from the yacht. Geroges thought you might like to have it back.'

'Yes.' Smoothing it out on her knee, she felt her eyes fill with tears and she looked hastily away from him.

'Drink your coffee, Verity,' he said gently, and he sounded as wretched as she felt. Sniffing hard, she put the hat on the table beside her and took the coffee from him.

'Thanks.'

'I'll make some soup for lunch, it will be easy for you to swallow. Is your throat still sore?'

'A bit,' she agreed. But it wasn't, not really, not from the retching anyway. It seemed blocked rather than sore. Choked.

The phone rang several times that morning, but Verity didn't ask who had called, nor did

Corbin volunteer the information. He made the soup, but after two spoonfuls Verity pushed the bowl away. She wasn't hungry. The day seemed to pass very slowly. Georges brought in a midday paper that had an account of the accident and the rescue. They'd spelt her name wrong, she saw, but it didn't matter. Nothing seemed to matter very much.

When she woke the next morning, she made a determined effort to be cheerful. It wasn't his fault. He'd never pretended to see her as more than as a friend, hadn't asked her to fall in love with him, and it was unfair to make him feel guilty by being miserable.

'Feeling better?' he asked hopefully, and she smiled warmly.

'Much better.'

'You still sound a bit husky.'

'Yes, from the wretched river water. I dread to think what I swallowed.' She didn't even dare consider if sewage went into it. If she dwelt on that, she thought she'd be sick again.

'Should you go to the hospital, do you think?' he asked worriedly. 'Just in case?'

'Heavens, no! I'll be OK. Truly. Stop worrying, Corbin.'

Nodding, his eyes still concerned, he asked with a determination that made her smile, 'What will you have to eat?'

'Eggs and bacon?' she asked, that being

the first thing that came into her head.

Smiling at her—obviously relieved that she wasn't going to be a problem, she thought wryly—he told her to go and sit in the lounge.

'I can do it, you know. I'm not ill.'

'No, I know,' he mumbled, his eyes growing shadowed again. 'Did you put the antiseptic cream that I left for you on your leg?'

'Yes, it's fine. Honestly.'

'All right, I'll go and cook some breakfast.'

Sitting in the lounge, she stared miserably into the fire. It was going to be an awful strain, trying to appear cheerful. When he called her for breakfast, she walked slowly out to the kitchen.

'The publisher rang about my book,' he murmured when they were seated.

'Oh, that's great, Corbin. I'm so glad,' she said with genuine warmth.

'You don't know what he said!' he exclaimed, laughing.

'Yes, I do. I bet he said it was great, terrific . . . Didn't he?' she asked softly.

'Well, something like that,' he mumbled, clearly embarrassed. 'He wants me to go and see him in London. Next week.'

'Then that's worked out very well, hasn't it?' she asked with forced enthusiasm. 'I shall be going back to work for David in a few weeks, and . . .'

'Where will you stay? With David and Mary?' he broke in.

'Maybe. Or maybe I'll get temporary lodgings. Oh, Corbin,' she exclaimed softly, aching for him, for the misery she was causing them both, 'you mustn't feel responsible for me. I'll be all right, really I will.'

'Yes, I know,' he sighed. 'It's just that—oh, hell, Verity, I feel so damned responsible!'

'Well, you mustn't,' she said firmly. Staring at him as he bent back to his breakfast, she examined the strong-boned face, the untidy mop of dark hair, and her eyes grew sad. Yet she wouldn't have missed knowing him, nor falling in love with him, really. At least she now knew herself capable of that emotion and, even if she never found anyone else, it was still something to be savoured. She would miss him dreadfully, she knew that, and there would be long, lonely nights when she would want him, but there had never been any question of him loving her. Sighing, she continued with her own meal.

They returned to England two days later. They drove to St Malo and got the ferry across to Portsmouth. Corbin had asked her if she'd prefer to fly, and she had considered it, for it would make a clean break from him. But foolishly, she'd decided to travel back with him, and savour the last few days. The weather in England didn't seem to be much improved on that in France. As they drove off the ferry, it was drizzling with rain, which continued all the way to London.

'Shall I drop you off at David's? He knows you're coming?'

'Yes. That will be fine. Thank you,' she said quietly.

He parked outside the house and killed the engine. Turning to face her, he stared at her for long moments, his expression bleak.

Summoning up a smile, she put out a gentle hand to touch his cheek. 'Goodbye, Corbin,' she said huskily. 'Take care, won't you?'

'Yes,' he murmured, his voice as husky as her own. 'Are you all right for money?'

'Yes.' With a shaky little sigh, she let her hand drop to her lap and turned to open the door. Protracted goodbyes would only make it harder.

He climbed out and opened the boot to take out her case and holdall, and they stood facing each other on the pavement, neither knowing quite what to say.

'Look after yourself,' he murmured.

'Yes. And you.'

'Yes. Goodbye, Verity—thank you for all you've done.'

Nodding, swallowing hard, she managed a wobbly smile as she felt tears prick her eyes. 'Bye.'

Jaw clenched, he swivelled on his heel and climbed quickly back into the car, and she watched it spurt away into the traffic. 'Bye,' she whispered thickly.

Taking a few moments to get herself under control, she then walked slowly up David's path. The door opened as she put her hand out to ring the bell.

'Hi,' she said with false lightness.

'Hi,' David said slowly, giving her a long, searching glance. 'Corbin gone?'

'Yes. He—er—had things to do. Did you manage to find me lodgings?'

'No,' he answered. 'You can stay here; there's no point finding somewhere just for a few weeks.'

'I asked you to find me digs,' she said obdurately.

'I know you did,' he responded amiably, then with a rather nasty gleam in his eye he added, 'You can tell me about it later—I have to go out. Or Mary can tell me later. Mary could get blood out of a stone.'

'There isn't anything to tell,' she said stiffly. 'Corbin finished his book, we came back to London, end of story. No dramas, nothing.'

'There never is with you.' He laughed. 'Everyone else has dramas, Verity just walks away. I could offer you the grossest insult, and you'd just walk away. Wouldn't you?' he asked softly.

'Don't be ridiculous! And if you're going out, hadn't you better go? You'll be late.'

Laughing, he yelled into the house, 'Mary? Verity's here. I'll see you later.' Grinning into Verity's cross face, he walked off whistling.

'Hi, Verity,' Mary greeted, taking the case and holdall from her. 'Come on into the kitchen. Hungry?'

'Not very, a sandwich will do. Why didn't David find digs for me?' she asked as she trailed Mary into the comfortable kitchen.

'Because we'd like you to stay here.' Mary smiled, pushing a large tabby cat off the rocking-chair and indicating Verity should sit. Then, peeking at her sideways, she asked, 'Going to tell me?'

'There's nothing to tell!' she said shortly. 'How many more times do I have to say it? Anyway, girlish confidences aren't my style.'

'You just ain't no fun, Verity Lang. No fun at all.'

'Then find me some digs.'

Laughing, Mary took the loaf out of the cupboard and proceeded to butter some slices. 'We read about the river rescue. Quite the heroine, aren't you?'

'No,' Verity answered shortly. 'And I don't want to talk about that, either.'

With an aggrieved sigh, Mary put slices of cheese between the bread and handed the plate to Verity. 'How's Corbin? I thought he might have come in with you.'

'Well, he didn't, and stop trying to provoke me, Mary. I won't rise.'

'No, I thought you might not.' And, her brown eyes speculative, Mary turned away to put the kettle on.

*　　　*　　　*

Despite her firm intention to find lodgings, both David and Mary blocked every move she made in that direction, and in the end she gave up. And maybe it was for the best: on her own she would probably have brooded, with David and Mary she was forced to make an effort to appear normal. It didn't stop her thinking about him, though. It seemed that every waking moment was spent in speculation about him. What he was doing, if he was happy with Eve. And if she cried into her pillow each night then there was no one to see, and if David or Mary heard her, or suspected, they weren't unkind enough to mention it.

By the middle of March, she thought she had maybe learned to live with it; she still ached, thought about him constantly, but she was coping. She was in her room one afternoon, desultorily sewing some buttons on a skirt, when Mary tapped at the door.

'You have a visitor,' she announced, and before Verity had time to even begin to speculate on who it might be Mary's slim form was replaced by Corbin's large one, and she just stared at him stupidly.

'Hello, Verity. May I come in?' he asked quietly, then did so before she answered, even if she could have found her tongue to do so, and closed the door softly behind him.

'How are you?'

'All right,' she whispered, her eyes still fixed rather blankly on his face. He looked tired, but familiarly rumpled: his hair was untidy, and his navy jumper looked as though it might be on back to front. He also looked as though he didn't quite know what to say.

'Are you busy?'

'No,' she said, her voice a mere breath of sound as she continued to stare at him.

'I missed you,' he said simply. 'I've been trying to screw up my courage to come and see you all week.'

'Have you?' She frowned. 'Why?'

'Because I discovered what a fool I was.'

'Fool?'

'Yes. All those months wasted, hankering after someone who wasn't worth the nail on your little finger. I had the gold, Verity—and I chose the dross.'

'Your eyes are blue today,' she said stupidly.

'What?'

'Blue,' she mumbled slowly, then moved her eyes to the sewing on her lap.

'Verity?'

Looking back at him, she gave a crooked smile. 'What did your publisher say?'

'It will come out some time next year——' he muttered impatiently. 'Verity, did you hear what I said?'

Nodding, she idly poked the needle through the button, and then just left it there, sticking out. 'Did you sleep with her?'

'No,' he said bluntly. 'I realised I could never want anyone but you.'

'Do you want to sleep with me, then?' she asked with a bluntness akin to his own.

'Oh, Verity——' he began helplessly.

'Do you?' she persisted.

With a long sigh, he admitted raggedly, 'Yes.'

Her lower lip trembling, she suddenly threw her sewing across the room and launched herself at him, and they both crashed backwards into the door. But his arms were holding her, a tight band across her ribs, and she hugged him fiercely, her eyes tight shut as she burrowed against his strong chest. 'Don't say anything,' she begged. 'Just hold me. Make love to me.'

'Now?'

'Now.'

Picking her up, he carried her to the bed and, laying her down, he lay beside her.

'Aren't we wearing too many clothes?' she whispered softly, her voice shaking.

'Are you sure, Verity?' he murmured thickly against her hair.

'I'm sure.'

'Not going to give me a hard time? Explanations, reasons . . .'

'Ssh,' she murmured, putting a hand across his mouth. 'I said, don't talk.'

Lifting his head, he framed her face with his palms and stared down into her eyes for a long moment, then with a little groan that reassured her more than any words could have done he lowered his mouth to hers.

They made love in silence, only their breathing and small groans disturbed the quiet in the room. Corbin led her gently, holding himself back, she guessed. His hands and mouth were sure, not hesitant, didn't pause or freeze when she gasped as he entered her, merely deepened the kiss, his fingers finding the sensitive points in her neck and shoulder so that she groaned and thrust against him. And then he was filling her, was part of her, and she sighed with pleasure, a warm feeling of love spreading through her body. Sliding her palms up his back to his neck, she whispered against his mouth, 'Oh, Corbin.'

'All right?' he asked softly, raising his head slightly to look down into her face.

'Yes.'

'Sore?'

'No. I expected it to hurt more than that,' she murmured in surprise. 'It's nice,' she added shyly, with a small, hesitant smile, and was surprised when his eyes darkened.

'Oh, Verity,' he groaned huskily. 'Oh, Verity!'

Trailing his mouth with exquisite slowness across her mouth to her neck and back again, his hands sought her breasts, his thumb probing the hardened nipple, and slowly, infinitely slowly, he moved his body on hers. Verity felt the muscles inside her expand and contract as her body matched its rhythm to his. Warmth spread through her, filled her heart, her mind; her blood quickened in her veins, her breathing accelerated to counterpoint with Corbin's. Unable to stop the cry that escaped her, she clenched her fingers on his back, moved them to his lower spine, pressed encouragingly, wrapped her legs round his, her body eager. She felt his hands slide to her buttocks, lift her, hold her as his movements became more urgent and his mouth captured hers again, his tongue thrusting intimately—an intrusion she welcomed with an abandonment that astonished her.

Locked together, they completed the spiral that defied analysis, sent mind and heart soaring, defied the laws of rationality. Their return to the small bedroom, to thought and feeling, was slow, gentle, exhausting. Dragging a deep breath into lungs that felt empty, Verity let it out on a shivering sigh and only slowly opened her eyes to stare at him. His weight was supported on his elbows, his eyes sleepy and dark, his hair tangled damply across his forehead.

'Oh, Verity,' he breathed, his voice barely audible. Then, with a funny little sound in his throat, he pressed his mouth to hers and rolled sideways, pulling her tight against his side. His chest rose and fell with jerky movements. The hands holding her so close, trembled.

'Will you forgive me?' he asked softly, his beautiful eyes shadowed.

'There's nothing to forgive,' she murmured, pushing his hair off his forehead, then allowing her hand to slide over the crown to rest against his nape. Nose to nose, they gazed into each other's eyes and, slowly, his filled with humour.

'Lovely Verity. Lovely, warm, generous Verity,' he sighed, his lips briefly touching hers.

'I love you,' she said simply.

'Yes. And I nearly threw it all away, didn't I?'

'Corbin!' she exclaimed, moving back a fraction. 'You're supposed to evince surprise, fervent gratitude . . .' He grinned unrepentantly.

Slapping him, she pulled her mouth down at the corners, her eyes laughing at him. 'But you knew how I felt, didn't you, back in Auray? You didn't need me to tell you the morning after the storm.'

I didn't know, exactly,' he said, his face serious. 'I didn't want to admit it, I think. I guessed you were maybe feeling more for me than you should that day I caught you on the stairs. That was a very bad mistake on my part. I couldn't get it out of my mind—thought I was going crazy. How could I want you when I was in love with Eve?'

'Did you want me, then?'

'Oh, yes. And that night after the storm when I held you in my arms. I wanted you very much, Verity.' Curving a strong hand behind her neck, he kissed her fiercely. 'You know one of the things I regretted most? That I might no longer be the first. Oh, Verity, I wanted so much for it to be me. Wished selfishly that I'd made love to you then. I can't believe now how blind I was, how stupid.'

'Does it matter so much to a man to be the first?' she asked, surprised. 'I would have thought, in this day and age . . .'

'It matters, Verity. It's so rare, so—oh, I don't know how to explain it, but yes, Verity, it matters an awful lot—makes a man feel special—and with all this women's lib, equality, there ain't much left to make a man feel special!'

'Was I . . .'

'Yes!' he laughed. 'You, my darling, are the only virgin I've—er—violated!'

'Corbin?' she asked thoughtfully, a small doubt in her mind.

'Mm?'

'Now that . . .'

'Now that I've had my wicked way with you, will I grow bored?' When she nodded, grateful for his understanding, he gave her a slow, beautiful smile. 'I can't envisage ever growing bored with you, darling. When we were living in Auray, if I came into the house and you weren't there, I felt lost, abandoned. I'd wander round touching things, picking them up, putting them down, then the minute

I heard your footsteps in the lane, I'd scoot into the study and pretend I'd been furiously working and not missed you at all. You were, are, comforting to have around—but certainly not boring! You make me feel peaceful, contented . . .'

'Even when we're shouting at each other?' she teased.

'Yes,' he agreed ruefully, 'even when we're shouting at each other. Didn't you find it added a rather sparky sort of excitement?' he murmured blandly, and Verity gave him a wry look.

'Yes, and look what it led to.'

'Nice though, isn't it?'

'Oh, yes,' she agreed softly. 'Very nice.'

'Stop sidetracking me,' he murmured, as she planted a lingering kiss on his chin. 'Eve didn't indulge in arguments, she'd just give a look of cold arrogance and walk off. With her, it was one damned intrigue after another, never knowing what sort of mood she'd be in. I never wanted to protect her, look after her the way I do with you. And yet in lots of ways you're much tougher than she is. One thing you must promise me, though—don't go jumping into any more rivers! I think I aged about ten years that day. I couldn't believe you hadn't drowned! I couldn't bear to lose you, Verity . . .' And his voice thickened, roughened, and she hugged him.

'Don't you realise that's how I felt when

I saw *you* dive in?' Shuddering, not wishing to remember that awful day, she rolled him on to his back, then leaned up on his chest to stare down into his strong face. His eyes looked grey now, she saw, but not cold. Most certainly not cold. Resting her chin on her linked hands, she demanded softly, 'Tell me how terrible she was, how selfish, how . . .'

Laughing, hugging her to him, he kissed her nose. 'I love you,' he said softly. 'Really love you. Deep inside. Not a surface attraction as it was with Eve, but deep in my heart, my mind. Oh, Verity, there's such a difference. I love you with a warmth, a passion, humour. Not illogically, against my will. But gladly, in a close, needing, delightful way. You're a very special lady.'

'Because I was a virgin?' she asked a trifle wistfully. It seemed an odd sort of reason to think her special. 'I wish I was beautiful for you.'

'You are beautiful,' he broke in gently. 'Beauty shines from your eyes, it shows in the curve of your delightful smile, your laugh, your beautiful glossy hair,' he went on, winding a long strand round his finger. 'You would be very hard to describe, I think. Your face doesn't stay still long enough to get a fair description. But you are beautiful—for me.'

Laying her face against his warm chest, she gave a long, contented sigh.

'Do you really want to talk about Eve?' he

asked.

'No. I'd rather talk about us. Corbin?'

'Mm?'

'Were the love scenes in the book based on you and Eve?'

'Eve?' he exclaimed incredulously. 'Good heavens, no! If you knew Eve better, you would realise what a preposterous question that is! Eve isn't a physical person. Not one to give you a hug when you were feeling blue. She had no intuition, could never read people's moods. To be honest, I don't know what attracted me to her. Her touch-me-not air, maybe—her air of mystery—which when you come down to it is just plain old indifference to anyone's feelings or opinions other than her own. I feel so damned stupid, pursuing a dream for so long—and why?' he demanded. 'I find the whole thing totally incomprehensible! I met her in London after we came back from France. I was still feeling as guilty as hell over you—and pretty miserable. I'd told myself so often that I was in love with her, that when I met her again I persuaded myself it had to be true. Yet the feelings she had always generated in me were no longer there.' Trailing a gentle finger along her nose, he smiled ruefully. 'I thought we weren't going to talk about her. Let's talk about when we first met.'

'On the other hand, why do we have to talk at all? I can think of lots of other things we could be doing,' she murmured naughtily as she slid her hand suggestively down his flat stomach.

'And you only newly instructed in the art, too!' he said, looking scandalised.

'I know, shocking, isn't it? But the books I've always read insist that at this point in time the—er—seducer murmurs something about it being much better the second time.'

'I thought it was pretty much all right the first time.' He grinned, kissing her delightful nose. 'However, if you insist . . .'

Giggling, she slapped his hand away. 'Go on with what you were saying.'

'Tease! I can't remember what I was saying. Yes, I can, I was going to tell you how astonished I was at my behaviour that first night in Auray when we were trying to sleep on the sofa. You'd been bad-tempered . . .'

'*We'd* been bad-tempered,' she corrected drily.

'All right, Miss Particular,' he laughed, 'We'd been bad-tempered, and I suddenly found myself wanting to tease you . . .'

'It was because I didn't know who you were, wasn't it? That was why you changed, relaxed.'

'Yes,' he admitted ruefully. 'I didn't know how much David had told you.' Sighing, he murmured, 'It had seemed such a long time since I'd laughed, teased anyone, wanted to be close to anyone. After Eve divorced me in the States, then the crash, I'd become a real old

grouch, and suddenly there was this Miss
Nobody answering me back, calling me
childish . . .' Laughing, he hugged her again.
'See how good you are for me? You ignore my
temper tantrums. You look after me . . .' He
tailed off with a bewildered look at her. 'Is
that what you want?' he frowned.

'Is that such a terrible ambition?' she asked
softly. 'To want to take care of you, make you
happy?'

'I don't know, Verity. It sounds incredibly
selfish, yet I find that's what I yearn for. Do
you really not have any ambitions? I'd hate to
think I'd stopped you doing something you
really wanted . . .' Suddenly he grinned. 'I just
remembered a conversation we had . . .'

'I know,' she murmured, totally attuned to
him, 'I said I only ever do what I want to do.
And what I want to do is stay with you, look
after you. Sounds dreadfully suburban,
doesn't it?' she grimaced. Staring at him, her
face suddenly troubled, she said quietly, 'Here
you are, a famous racing driver, with a life-
style I can probably only guess at, and here am
I, cosily pushing you into a life of domesticity . . .'

'It sounds wholly delightful,' he responded.
'I've always envied people that,' he added
softly, 'pictures of their family on their desks,
gap-toothed children grinning out of the
frame. Whenever I've stayed with Pete and his
wife, and their two small children, seen how

they live, it's made my life seem very shallow. For a long time there'd been only Stella—and Eve was hardly an advertisement for cosy domesticity, she was always wanting to go out, be seen.' Snuggling her down into his shoulder, he continued happily, 'We'll get married, you and I, raise a family, and live contentedly ever after.'

'Can we have a cottage in the country? And dogs? All the trimmings?' she teased. 'It sounds a very odd sort of thing to want, doesn't it? Everyone else I know strives for interesting jobs, to be heads of industry, fashion designers, and all I want is to look after you.'

'That's an interesting job,' he laughed, tipping her up and leaning on one elbow to look down into her face. 'I personally would call it the most interesting, challenging job of all time.'

'Oh, definitely.' She grinned. 'Did you decide what you were going to do about racing?'

'Mm, I think so. As I told Pete, I no longer have the necessary edge of aggression. See? You've tamed the tiger.'

'Oh, Corbin,' she exclaimed, worried, 'please don't give it up because of me. I couldn't bear to be the cause of . . .'

'Hush,' he said, putting a gentle hand across her mouth, 'I've had an approach to commentate on the Grand Prix and, if I accepted that, maybe do some more writing . . .'

'But won't you miss it? I shan't mind—yes,
I shall, of course I shall. I shall be worried sick
if you race, but if it's what you want . . .'

'No. Oh, I shall probably miss it at first,
miss the adrenalin, the excitement, the smell of
diesel; it was a major part of my life for a long
time. But I have the world championship, I've
achieved what I set out to achieve.' Smiling
warmly at her, he murmured, 'Love me?'

'Oh, yes, lots and lots,' she said fervently.

'Then make love to me,' he whispered
softly. 'I think I need you very badly.' Then, a
humorous twinkle appearing in his eyes, he
added, 'Did you remember you left your
father's picture in my car?'

'Yes. Did you bring it with you?'

'No. I hung it in the flat. You see how
devious I can be? If you wouldn't forgive me,
then at least I would have a chance to inveigle
you into my home . . .'

'Did you really think I wouldn't welcome
you with open arms? I didn't expect to see you
again. Kept tormenting myself with images of
you and Eve——'

'Enough,' he murmured. 'No more talking.'
Wrapping her warmly in his arms, he made
love to her with slow enjoyment, his mouth
and hands proving quite conclusively just how
much he did love and need her—and Verity
responded with an unashamed fervour that
delighted him.

Lying quietly, entwined in each other's arms, Corbin ran warm palms up and down her back until she gave a little shiver.

'Cold?' he asked, concerned.

'No. But I suppose we ought to make a move. David and Mary must have chewed their nails to the elbows by now. Come on, lazybones, let's go and have a shower . . .'

'Together?' he exclaimed, sounding so scandalised that she collapsed in giggles. 'Good heavens, Verity, are you sure I'm ready for these new-fangled ideas? What happened to modesty?'

'What happened to chastity?' she asked wryly.

'Oh, hell, I suppose you'll *have* to marry me now you've so thoroughly compromised me . . .'

When they went downstairs, hand in hand, Mary grinned and winked, while David just looked at them, hands placed rather aggressively on his hips.

'No,' he said bluntly. 'You cannot have her . . .' And Verity choked and bit her lip. 'Verity!' he said sternly. 'Behave yourself.'

'Sorry,' she said meekly, 'but it's all right, David, I wouldn't dream of leaving you in the lurch.'

'Yes, she would.' Corbin grinned. 'She's going to marry me as soon as I can arrange a licence.'

'Then you'd better arrange it pretty damned quick, because we go to Rome in exactly two weeks.'

'We could honeymoon in Rome,' she put in hastily as she felt Corbin stiffen. 'Find an apartment. Would you mind so very much, Corbin? I can't let David down. You could write just as easily in Rome, couldn't you?'

'I could,' he agreed. 'I'm not terribly sure I want to. Rome in the summer can be horrendous . . .'

'But possible,' David put in triumphantly. 'The bank would defray some of the costs of the apartment . . .'

'And you could start looking for someone else straight away . . .' Corbin taunted with a rather nasty smile.

'I could—but I'm not altogether sure I want to . . .

'Stop it, you two,' Mary put in, coming to stand between the two men. 'And it's your own fault, David. You were the one who said Verity would be perfect for him . . .

'I didn't mean as his wife!'

'Aren't you just the teeniest bit pleased for me?' Verity asked with a winning smile.

'Oh, Verity,' he sighed, 'of course I am— I'm delighted for you both.' Walking across to her, he gave her a hug, then slapped Corbin rather too forcefully on the back.

'Don't dislocate his spine,' Mary reproved. 'By the look in Verity's eyes, he's going to

need to be in very good working order. She has
a lot of time to make up——'

'Mary!' Verity spluttered, then, laughing,
she hugged Corbin's arm to her. 'Not that
she's entirely wrong . . .' she murmured with a
devilish little grin.

'Then we'd best be going,' Corbin said
firmly. 'We have a lot of things to do and not
much time to do them in.'

'Where are we going?' she asked, bewildered.

'To my flat, of course, so that I can have my
evil way with you—in private!'

Take 4 bestselling love stories FREE

Plus get a FREE surprise gift!

PASSPORT TO ROMANCE
SWEEPSTAKES RULES

1   **HOW TO ENTER:** To enter, you must be the age of majority and complete the official entry form, or print your name, address, telephone number and age on a plain piece of paper and mail to: Passport to Romance, P.O. Box 9056, Buffalo, NY 14269-9056. No mechanically reproduced entries accepted.

2   All entries must be received by the CONTEST CLOSING DATE, DECEMBER 31, 1990 TO BE ELIGIBLE.

3   **THE PRIZES:** There will be ten (10) Grand Prizes awarded, each consisting of a choice of a trip for two people from the following list:
    i)   London, England (approximate retail value $5,050 U.S.)
    ii)   England, Wales and Scotland (approximate retail value $6,400 U.S.)
    iii) Carribean Cruise (approximate retail value $7,300 U.S.)
    iv)   Hawaii (approximate retail value $9,550 U.S.)
    v)   Greek Island Cruise in the Mediterranean (approximate retail value $12,250 U.S.)
    vi)   France (approximate retail value $7,300 U.S.)

4   Any winner may choose to receive any trip or a cash alternative prize of $5,000.00 U.S. in lieu of the trip.

5   **GENERAL RULES:** Odds of winning depend on number of entries received.

6   A random draw will be made by Nielsen Promotion Services, an independent judging organization, on January 29, 1991, in Buffalo, NY, at 11:30 a.m. from all eligible entries received on or before the Contest Closing Date.

7   Any Canadian entrants who are selected must correctly answer a time-limited, mathematical skill-testing question in order to win.

8   Full contest rules may be obtained by sending a stamped, self-addressed envelope to: "Passport to Romance Rules Request", P.O. Box 9998, Saint John, New Brunswick, Canada E2L 4N4.

9   Quebec residents may submit any litigation respecting the conduct and awarding of a prize in this contest to the Régie des loteries et courses du Québec.

10 Payment of taxes other than air and hotel taxes is the sole responsibility of the winner.

11 Void where prohibited by law

COUPON BOOKLET OFFER TERMS

To receive your Free travel-savings coupon booklets, complete the mail-in Offer Certificate on the preceeding page, including the necessary number of proofs-of-purchase, and mail to: Passport to Romance, P.O. Box 9057, Buffalo, NY 14269-9057. The coupon booklets include savings on travel-related products such as car rentals, hotels, cruises, flowers and restaurants. Some restrictions apply. The offer is available in the United States and Canada. Requests must be postmarked by January 25, 1991. Only proofs-of-purchase from specially marked "Passport to Romance" Harlequin® or Silhouette® books will be accepted. The offer certificate must accompany your request and may not be reproduced in any manner. Offer void where prohibited or restricted by law. LIMIT FOUR COUPON BOOKLETS PER NAME, FAMILY, GROUP, ORGANIZATION OR ADDRESS. Please allow up to 8 weeks after receipt of order for shipment. Enter quickly as quantities are limited. Unfulfilled mail-in offer requests will receive free Harlequin® or Silhouette® books (not previously available in retail stores), in quantities equal to the number of proofs-of-purchase required for Levels One to Four, as applicable.

OFFICIAL SWEEPSTAKES ENTRY FORM

Complete and return this Entry Form immediately—the more Entry Forms you submit, the better your chances of winning!
- Entry Forms must be received by **December 31, 1990**
- A random draw will take place on **January 29, 1991**
- Trip must be taken by **December 31, 1991**

3-HP-3-SW

YES, I want to win a PASSPORT TO ROMANCE vacation for two! I understand the prize includes round-trip air fare, accommodation and a daily spending allowance.

Name_____

Address_____

City_____ State_____ Zip_____

Telephone Number_____ Age_____

Return entries to: **PASSPORT TO ROMANCE**, P.O. Box 9056, Buffalo, NY 14269-9056

© 1990 Harlequin Enterprises Limited

COUPON BOOKLET/OFFER CERTIFICATE

Item	LEVEL ONE Booklet 1	LEVEL TWO Booklet 1 & 2	LEVEL THREE Booklet 1, 2 & 3	LEVEL FOUR Booklet 1, 2, 3 & 4
Booklet 1 = $100+	$100+	$100+	$100+	$100+
Booklet 2 = $200+		$200+	$200+	$200+
Booklet 3 = $300+			$300+	$300+
Booklet 4 = $400+	____	____	____	$400+
Approximate Total Value of Savings	$100+	$300+	$600+	$1,000+
# of Proofs of Purchase Required	4	6	12	18
Check One	____	____	____	____

Name_____

Address_____

City_____ State_____ Zip_____

Return Offer Certificates to: **PASSPORT TO ROMANCE**, P.O. Box 9057 Buffalo, NY 14269-9057

Requests must be postmarked by **January 25, 1991**

✂ -

 ONE PROOF OF PURCHASE   3-HP-3

To collect your free coupon booklet you must include the necessary number of proofs-of-purchase with a properly completed Offer Certificate

© 1990 Harlequin Enterprises Limited

See previous page for details